BEAR WITH ME

NICOLE BLANCHARD

Bear With Me

Copyright © 2021 by Nicole Blanchard

Publisher's Note: This is a work of fiction. Names, characters, places, and incidents are a product of the author's imagination. Locales and public names are sometimes used for atmospheric purposes. Any resemblance to actual people, living or dead, or to businesses, companies, events, institutions, or locales is completely coincidental.

Dedication

To Mom

Contents

Chapter One
Sully

I t wasn't until I lost my parents in a car accident that I learned about the gift I inherited from my mother. The gift that changed everything I thought I knew about myself and my family.

Sometimes, I even manage to forget the new powers I possess, until I touch something, anything, and am bombarded by memories. I can't very well pull away from my brother's outstretched hand as he passes a packing box to me to load into the truck, so I brace myself and wince as I'm bombarded by his thoughts and memories.

I wonder if there will be any hot girls there.

I wish Sully would talk to me like we used to.

There better be enough gas in this thing to make it a couple hours north at least.

As he thinks about the truck, an image flashes through my mind of the day my parents brought home the truck for his sixteenth birthday, only I'm seeing and feeling everything from Sam's point of view. I can even see my glowing, smiling face in the background.

A gasp wrenches from my chest and I jerk away, rubbing my hands together to rid myself of the remnants from the vision. They leak from my mind like sand in an hourglass and I refocus on Sam's concerned face in front of me.

"Hey, you okay?"

I hate that question. I must have been asked it a thousand times since the night we lost our parents. As a result, I bite out, "I'm fine," with more force than necessary. I immediately regret it when his face falls and I want to say something to apologize, but there are no words left.

How do I tell him what's happened to me? How do I even do that without sounding crazy?

Before I can offer an explanation, he's slamming the back door and loping to the driver's seat. I sigh and lift my thick brown hair off of my shoulders. I'm looking forward to cooler weather in Indiana.

As he pulls away from the curb of the home we spent our entire lives in, I keep my eyes on its shrinking form in the rearview mirror. I wish I'd been given the power to control time instead of... whatever it is I have. At least it would allow me to do something useful.

Like save my parents.

Instead, the only thing I have are memories. All of them, it seems. It doesn't matter if it's a person or an inanimate object. If I touch it, I see everything about it. Like a history lesson I wish I could ignore as easily as I had my seventh period AP class senior year.

It's no wonder my mom was so eerily in tune with us.

For a while I thought maybe Sam had gotten it, too. I'd even tried bringing it up at the funeral, but he only looked at me like I was crazy.

I didn't bring it up again.

As I leave everything I've ever known behind, I wonder if I'll ever start to feel like the girl I was before my life fell apart. I touch the window in farewell as our house disappears from view. A tear leaks from the corner of my eye and even in my sorrow, the memory of Sam making out with his ex-girlfriend fills my thoughts. I jerk my hand away, rubbing it on my jeans and groaning. That was definitely not an image I want burned into my brain. I force myself to relax and fall asleep. I manage to do so somewhere around Mississippi.

"Wake up, we're almost there," Sam says.

I peel myself off of the center console and look out into a different world. Florida doesn't have time for seasons like fall or winter. There's barely a drop in temperature before the sun comes back, brighter than ever.

Somehow we made it to Indiana without killing each other. Farmland and palm trees were replaced with full, towering oaks. Beach and sand with thick, vibrant woods. And endless country roads with a quaint little town nestled at the edge of a massive national forest.

I watch Sam out of the corner of my eye as his aviator sunglasses flash and his lips, identical to my own, mouth along with the pop song on the radio. A few months ago, I would have been singing along with him—we made the perfect duet. Call it twintuition or whatever. Now I don't even have the energy to mouth the words.

"C'mon, Sully. It's your favorite song," Sam says beside me. He only calls me Sully when he's trying to be particularly pitiful. Normally it makes me smile, but this time it doesn't. I feel...nothing. Inside, I am empty and raw. I tug on my mother's locket and a wisp of her face appears, but it's faint, almost transparent. Maybe there's a limited number of times I can revisit a memory.

The thought makes me ache. "Don't call me that," I say as I stare at the passing scenery. Just hearing that name now makes me want to explode.

The last time he called me Sully was the night our parents died. I was laying on my bed in the soft, dreamy space between awake and unconsciousness. My earbuds were crooning a sweet song, and I was entirely relaxed. Then, I shot straight up in bed, my heart beating double time in my chest. At first, I thought it was one of those dreams where you're falling, but wake up just before you *splat* on the ground. But it wasn't. A knock came at my door and my head jerked in its direction to find Sam in the doorway. The look on his face told me it wasn't a dream. That what was coming was the stuff of nightmares. The racing heart was because he felt it, too.

I relaxed a little just knowing he was there. "You scared me," I told him.

When he didn't crack a joke or even a smile, I pulled out the earbuds. "Something wrong? Did you and Lena have another fight?" She was the cheerleading captain to his quarterback. They were notorious for their on-again off-again relationship. "Mom and Dad home?"

It was their twentieth anniversary and he'd taken her out to their favorite restaurant to celebrate. I made fun of them when they were leaving for how sappy they were about it, but inside I loved the way their eyes caught each other from across the room or when my dad stopped what he was doing just to kiss her silly.

"Sully," Sam started, then paused to swallow, his Adam's apple bobbing. "Sully, Mom and Dad were in accident. The police are here. They didn't make it."

Didn't make it.

After that it was a blur of funeral arrangements, concerned friends and family, and an abundance of lawyers. In a moment my life changed. Before I was on the track to Columbia, to practice law, like my father. And just like that, I could no longer afford to go there, not with the astronomical costs of closing my parents' estate and the price of school alone.

When Nonna, our maternal grandmother, called and offered us a spot at the small university in her town, I wasn't left with many other options. As a donor to Hastings-Albrecht University, our grandmother was able to buy our way into the school. It wasn't a bad place to go to school, it was just no Columbia. Indiana felt like it was a universe away from my former life.

Aside from taking the edge off of Sam's whip-like humor, he didn't seem much worse for the wear. Then again, of the two of us, he had always been the more upbeat one. When we were kids, he was the magician, the trickster, and the goof. Not much had changed as he got older, except all of his tricks seemed to have turned to charm somehow because the girls flocked to him.

On him, the strong jaw, full lips and striking blue eyes made his face interesting and unique. Women were always turning around to give him a second look and he was most at home in a crowd. I had never been as confident about my body as he was. Instead of accentuating it, I went without makeup and cute hairstyles, preferring to stick with my ponytails and loose clothes. I was much more comfortable on my own with my nose stuck in a book.

"Okay, *Sullivan.*" Sam punches the volume button on the radio and an uncomfortable silence fills the tense space between us.

We lapse into silence as we pass the Welcome to Hillsborough sign and roll onto Main Street. My eyes catch on the news station which houses the

Hillsborough Chronicle where I'll be helping out as an assistant after classes.

"Dude," Sam exclaims, his head twisting around, "I think I just saw an eagle."

Without lifting my head, I reply, "It's probably just a buzzard, jackass. Keep your eye on the road."

"Don't let Granny Suzanna hear you talking like that."

"I'm eighteen and she's not my mother," I state firmly, then I lift my head and quirk a brow at him. "I would love to hear you call Nonna 'Granny Suzanna.'"

He smiles at me and I catch myself smiling back instinctually. A beat passes and my smile falls. Noting that, Sam's lips press together and he swings his head back toward the road. A rift has grown between us, full of all the things I can't tell him and all the things he doesn't understand. We're out of sync. On different wavelengths. Dancing to different songs.

It's almost as bad as losing him along with my parents.

Even worse because I can fix it, but I don't know how.

Nonna's house is in the well-to-do section of Hillsborough. Sam pulls the truck to a stop by the curb where it is decidedly out of place amongst the BMWs. He bounds out of the truck and up a concrete walkway bordered by a lush garden in full bloom. I don't know what kind of architecture the house—mansion really—is, but it rises in an impressive sprawl on the top of the hill. Nonna's family was one of the founders of Hillsborough. My mom never went into details and her voice sharpened whenever I tried to get to know her parents more.

Considering my new abilities, I'm starting to understand why. If I inherited it from my mother, she must have gotten it from hers.

I pause on the walkway to stare at the three-story monstrosity. My parents had vastly simpler tastes. My childhood home was a tasteful ranch-style that had weathered the test of time. Complete with toddler drawings in hidden corners and our growth charts scribbled on the bathroom door frames.

Sam knocks on the front door. There's a short pause before the door opens to reveal Nonna, dressed impeccably in a linen suit, her dyed brown hair perfectly coiffed. She wraps her arms around him, the expensive-looking bracelets on her wrists jangling together. I move forward reluctantly, the wheels of my suitcase catching on the cracks in the concrete behind me.

I'd left the pieces of my home—and some of me—behind. Gorgeous though it may be, the building in front of me feels like a stranger's house. And I want nothing more than to turn around and head back where we came from.

"Wow!" Sam says from inside the foyer. "This place is massive. You must really be rolling in it, huh?"

I roll my eyes at him and clamber up the front steps, feeling awkward with my bulky suitcase dragging along. Nonna's eyes study me, no doubt taking in my wrinkled shirt and cutoff jean shorts which are a far cry from elegant. I hug her, taking care not to make any contact with my hands. She smells like my mother, lavender and talc, but I have no desire to delve into her memories.

"I'm so glad you could make it, Sullivan." She pulls back so that she can look me over. "You look just like your mother when she was your age."

"Yeah, um, I get that a lot." I wind my hair with my fingers and peer past her into the house where Sam is already exploring. "You have a beautiful home," I manage to say.

"Thank you. It's been in our family since the first Thomas settled in Hillsborough." She takes a step back and gestures inside. "Why don't you come in?"

I offer a brittle smile and wheel my suitcase over the bump in the doorway. A staircase to my immediate left leads to the second story and just in front of me is a sunken living room with a large dark leather sectional. On the other side, a pair of French doors lead out to the back yard. The space is airy and comfortable.

As I set my suitcase next to the stairs, I rest my hand on the banister for the barest of moments. It doesn't take any longer than that for the memory to wash over me.

I see my mother around my age, and damn if she doesn't look just like me. She's rushing around the house in a flurry of movement, stuffing things into her own suitcase. Nonna stands in the background, her arms crossed over her chest and a stormy look over her younger features.

The moment fades out and present day fades back in with Nonna watching me with knowing eyes. I snatch my hand off of the banister and say, "Do you mind showing me the room? I'm a bit worn out from the drive."

"Really, Sullivan? You slept the whole way here. If anyone should be tired, it's me," Sam says, coming to stand beside us.

I give him a look that says to mind his own business before Nonna tries to play referee. "Of course. You both must be exhausted. Dinner won't be ready for a couple hours yet."

"This used to be your mom's room," Nonna says from the doorway a few minutes later as I take a few tentative steps forward. Her admission causes ice to form in my chest and I pause to look around.

Unlike my room in Florida, this one looks as though it's been preserved since my mom left. The cream walls and white furniture are accented with pastel pink drapes and bedding. Nothing like my own, more earthy style. I can almost picture her sitting at the desk, her face brightened with a smile.

I tear away from that image and force myself to look around the rest of the room. The Jack and Jill bath next to the walk-in closet leads to Sam's room, where he's already sprawled across his own bed. He doesn't look up when I enter and I figure he's already passed out.

I return to my room and smile hesitantly at Nonna. "Thank you again for letting us stay. And, you know, for school."

Nonna nods, a movement so reminiscent of my mother it causes my chest to squeeze. "We stick together in this town, sweetie. You'll learn to love it."

"Maybe." I turn to unpack my bags.

"You know," comes her hesitant voice over my shoulder. "If you ever want to...talk about anything. I'm here. I know we haven't been close, but I hope this opportunity will change that. I would like to get to know you and your brother."

I swallow the lump in my throat, but manage to smile. "Sure, that would be great."

She opens her mouth like she wants to say something and then closes it again. She looks around the room, her eyes lingering like mine had, probably imaging Mom. "I know you're going to have questions. About... things. You can come to me. If you need someone to talk to, I mean."

My heart thuds loudly in my chest. A million questions begging answers war in my mind and somehow constrict like a tangle of snakes in my throat. The moment passes and she nods regally and leaves.

The fight drains from me and my feet buckle. I slump to the bed as Sam's snores echo from the next room.

So she does know about my gift.

Heat prickles the hairs at the back of my neck—and not in a pleasant warm-afternoon kind of way. In the uncomfortable, I-feel-completely-out-of-place kind of way. The voices of the librarian and her male friend are low with intimacy. One that makes my insides burn with jealousy and annoyance.

I'd kill for some kind of interruption at this point, but it's summer term, so the library is as empty as a tomb. She lets out a low laugh and my shoulders raise up in an attempt to block out the seduction scene going on behind me.

For the first time since I gained these *abilities*, I'm happy for the constant hum of voices coming from layer after layer of psychic babble from the tabletop and the mouse I'm using to browse through available summer classes.

When I realized my perfect dreams had been shot, I pretty much gave up the idea of ever getting the kind of life I wanted. Sounds dramatic, but it was easier than focusing on what was really going on. Now that I'm actually here, I feel that familiar excitement of possibilities thrumming just beneath my skin. Or maybe that's the dregs of memories I'm absorbing from the keyboard. Either way, as I shuffle through the registration process, a seed of hope takes root in my chest.

The woman gasps behind me and I do my best to ignore as I worry over whether or not to push off my one and only math class until next semester. I don't want to overload myself, but what the hell. I have nothing better to do, so I add it to my list with the journalism elective and general biology.

While the list is printing for my records, I gather my purse and cell up from the desk. A weight eases from my chest now that I've got some sort of goals to work toward. Something to keep me busy.

I'm so distracted by the thought of a new start that I accidentally let my fingers brush the woman's as I hand her the registration form. When our fingers make contact, I can't help my sudden gasp. In an instant it goes from mid-afternoon to evening. The low moans I'd been hearing increase in volume as the scene before me materializes.

The couple doesn't notice me, which is probably a good thing considering how wrapped up in each other they are. My breath catches in my throat and a flush spreads over my body. He's got her pinned against the counter, his hands delving beneath the material of her shirt.

She moans and so do I, and damn if I can't feel his fingers undoing the claps of my own bra. I go from zero to sixty in a couple seconds flat, bordering on an edge of a heatwave. I pull my hand back to grip something, anything, and the vision fades away, leaving me gasping for breath like a fish out of water.

I manage to get myself under control, barely, and look up to find the two of them looking at me like I've lost my mind. Caught between arousal and embarrassment, I squeak out a "Thank you" and then get the hell out of there.

The fresh air does little to soothe the burn on my cheeks. I imagine that every person can feel the pulse beating low in my stomach. That they can see it on my face. There isn't enough acreage on this lush campus to put enough distance between me and that scene.

I stumble upon a little café in the center of campus and I order up a French vanilla cappuccino in the hopes that it will erase the pounding behind my eyes. Around me students are paired off into groups already and a haunting sense of loneliness grows in my stomach.

With the scene I just witnessed fresh in my mind, I take extra care to keep my hands from brushing against anyone else. The last thing I need is someone else's sex life taking up residence in my head. It's a sad, visceral reminder that I have no sex life of my own. Kind of hard to get down and dirty when you can hear every thought from a simple touch.

I weave through the crowd to an empty bistro table and plop down with a sound of relief. With registration finished, I finally have some control back in my life. I may not understand what's happening to me or where I go from here about Nonna and Sam, but at least I have this. The coffee is exactly what I need and I groan through the first caffeinated sip.

A pair of hands cover my eyes and a familiar voice says, "Guess who?" in my ear.

"Really, Sam? Are we ten?"

"Hey," he responds, his eyes still on the ladies trolling around us, "I don't know about you, but I find my childlike enthusiasm entertaining."

"Yeah, keep telling yourself that." But I can't help the smile that spreads. "So what do you need? Are you ready to head back to Nonna's?" There's a good book and a comfortable bed with my name on it. I figure outside of classes I can read myself into a coma.

Sam puts all four legs of the wrought iron chair down and manages to tear his attention away from the ladies. "So, you know you love me, right? Most times, I mean."

"Ye-e-s? Did you get into some kind of trouble already? Dammit, Sam."

He holds up a hand. "Wow, what a show of faith, I'm hurt Sully. Really hurt."

I roll my eyes. "What do you want?" And I'm so distracted I forget to be pissed about him calling me Sully.

"Well there's this thing tonight."

"Thing?"

"This huge party they have every year. Some kind of summer festival. The whole town goes."

"So? What do you need me for?"

"To protect me. The women here," he looks off into the distance smiling fondly, "they're animals."

"I think you can handle yourself."

"So you're going to leave me to the wolves?"

I take a drink so I can compose my answer. "I don't know, Sam. We don't know anyone here."

"That's the point. I know you don't want to talk about Mom and Dad, so I won't, but you have got to get out of the house. Live a little. So I want you to go to this thing with me. Have a little fun. What could it hurt?"

Famous last words.

Chapter Two
Sully

The moment we arrive I can tell I sorely miscalculated this "festival". Everyone else is in jeans and T-shirts while I hop out of the truck in a dress Sam said would be fine. That's the last time I'll ever take his advice. I glare at him, but he doesn't notice, not with a party going on, the social butterfly that he is. He definitely got all of the extrovert genes when we shared a womb.

The bastard. He could have at least shared.

He looks back towards me for permission and I sigh, knowing that he won't be able to stay glued by my side no matter how much I want him to. "Go ahead," I tell him.

Sam grins and for a moment the pain that's a mirror of my own melts from his face. Seeing that, knowing that he hides his more easily than I do, I'm glad I decided to come with him. No one else but me can see the sadness that pulls the light from his eyes or the pallor his complexion has taken due to lack of sleep. Some of it, I put there, and he doesn't deserve that.

I tilt my cheek up to receive his kiss on my cheek. "I'll see you later." He backs away smiling.

Then I'm left alone, but I put on a brave face. If he can do this, then so can I.

From the way he described it, I thought this was supposed to be some sort of town fair of sorts. With vendors and bouncy houses. I was wrong.

This is a college party complete with kegs, bonfires, and tailgates. Groups of beautiful looking people are bunched together clasping red plastic cups, their cheeks already ruddy with alcohol. No one seems to pay any mind to the growing darkness or the looming threat of rain.

Sam has already found himself a group of girls to charm and based on his laugh, I made the right choice in coming with him. Seeing him happy lifts my spirits, so I slog across the field to the keg, my delicate lace ballet flats taking a beating. I don't plan on drinking much, if any, but I need something to keep my hands busy.

Cup in hand, I navigate through the crowd, hoping to spot a kind face. Instead, I run smack into a group of rowdy frat guys whose eyes collectively brighten at my presence.

"Oh," one says, as the fire throws harsh shadows over his normally handsome face, "look what we have here." People don't really sound like villains in an after school special, do they? My luck I'd find some slime bucket straight off.

I back away, but not before he puts his hands on my arm, his grip inescapable. I use my free hand to try and push him away, stealing myself against the contact. "Sorry, excuse me."

"Not so fast there, sweetheart."

I'm in no way used to having the thoughts of others invade my mind, but I assumed I'd grown accustomed enough that their innermost desires didn't shock me anymore. The mundane, the obnoxious and everything in between. But I'd never experienced something as insidious as this guy's thoughts.

I recoil, jerking my hand roughly, probably bruising the flesh of my wrist, but I don't care. Anything to get away from his touch. "Let me go."

When he doesn't and his little friends make no effort to help me, I pull back my free arm and punch him square in the nose. The satisfying crunch causes him to drop his hold on me and I take a few hasty steps backward. Relief is short lived.

So much for making friends here tonight.

Thunder rumbles and the roar from the crowd brings back the pulsing behind my eyes. I lose myself in the throng of bodies, putting as much distance between me and the jerk as possible. I'll find somewhere quiet to hide until Sam has had his fun. Beer still in hand, I ease my way back through the crush of people and take solace in the emptiness of the woods. The tension stringing me up tight loosens the moment I step beyond the trees.

Swift River National Park borders the town of Hillsborough and from what I understand it's huge. I make sure to keep the party in my sight and manage to find a cluster of rocks where I climb up and sit while sipping my beer. There's a thick section of trees that separates me from all the other people.

It's not lost on me this is how I feel most of the time since my parents' deaths. Separated. Apart. Alone. Other. It's like my life forked off into Before and After. Before they died I'd been a normal teenager, getting ready for my freshman year of college, looking forward to starting my life as an adult. Full of possibilities, with boundless opportunities. After, I became isolated by the cursed gift I received without warning, adrift on a current of fear and desperation.

I drink deeply from my cup. No more self pity. This move is a chance to start fresh. Soon, the sound of the distant party and the distant sound of animals in the woods lull away the encounter with the jerk and my nerves settle.

Twigs snap behind me and my spine straightens. I squint through the growing darkness. "Who's there?" I ask, lifting a hand to my eyes and squinting. My heart beats double time and I wonder if maybe punching that asshole hadn't been the smartest move.

All too belatedly I realize I shouldn't have gone so far from the crowd. If something were to happen to me, no one would be able to hear me scream.

The shadows shift and part to reveal the biggest man I've ever seen. The kind of man that sends a thrill of warning down my back. He's dressed in jeans that have seen their fair share of toil. Definitely not the expensive designer ones that Sam prefers. A simple white t-shirt and flannel cover his broad shoulders, the sleeves are rolled up to reveal forearms corded with thick muscles. He doesn't seem like the type to hit the gym. No this is a man who built his muscle through sheer physical effort. A beard frames his full lips and disappears into the beanie covering his head. Dark hair peeks out from the vee in his shirt and the feminine parts of me tighten.

He's not a boy like the one I'd just run from. This guy is all man. Too old for this crowd, for sure. Too old for me, definitely. What was he doing out here?

"Didn't mean to scare you," he says and I shiver. Not from cold or fear, but from a pure rush of desire. His voice is pure warmth and I feel it like a wave of heat from a crackling fire.

I glance back towards the line of trees and note that they're too far away for me to make a dash. He could catch me, if that's what he wants. From the way his assessing amber eyes follow me, studying, I get the feeling that he's calculating every move and I have no doubt that he could snatch me up in seconds, even considering his bulk.

"You didn't scare me," I say with more confidence than I feel. "Just wasn't expecting anyone else to be out here. I figured everyone would all be up at the party."

He leans a big shoulder up against the trunk of a tree. "There are all kinds of things out in these woods, especially at night. You'd probably be best back over there with the rest of them."

Laughter trails through the thick brush and I

spot the guy who grabbed me. I am unable to suppress a shudder at the memory—his memories. "I'm okay out here."

He straightens and moves to go, then pauses, his bottom lip sucked between his teeth. Heat unfurls low in my stomach and my breath hitches. I can feel his eyes on me like a predator waiting to stake claim on his prey.

"I'm not going to lie to you, I saw him grab you and I followed you out here. Wanted to make sure you were okay." He glances back at him, then raises an eyebrow at me. "Clearly you handled yourself."

I shrug and wrap my arms around myself against the bite of chill in the air. "I've got a twin brother so I'm fairly used to male stupidity."

The first drops of rain begin to fall and I shiver. I'm going to kill Sam for dragging me out here. I scan the crowds, but don't see his familiar face, just a sea of unfamiliar ones.

He takes a couple steps toward me, shrugging out of his flannel button up and laying it over my shoulders. A groan very nearly escapes from my lips, but I swallow it down. The warmth and scent of him wraps around me like a blanket. Having him so close to me causes the heat in my stomach to ignite.

"I'm Declan," he says, holding out a hand. It's

sexy, as far as hands go. Big palms and thick fingers. It looks harmless enough, but I know what secrets lie behind such a seemingly innocent touch.

Even knowing there's a horrible possibility in returning the gesture, I fit my much smaller hand in his. I brace myself for the onslaught and I nearly fall off of the rock when I see...nothing.

Absolutely nothing.

My eyes lift to his in shock and I forget to release his hand. I know there's no way I've lost the gift so quickly, not when flashes of that jerk's memories still surface every few seconds like a bad nightmare.

"Gonna tell me yours?" he asks and at first I think he's talking about *my* secrets.

When I realize he means my name, and I finally have enough brain cells under control to answer, I release his hand and stutter out, "Sullivan. Sully," I add without thinking.

"Nice to meet you, Sully." He sits next to me on the rock. "What brings you to Hillsborough?"

"An accident," I answer. "You?"

"I was born here and just never left."

The rain starts coming down harder and my clothes are soaked within seconds. "Do people in this town often have parties in the middle of a storm?"

Declan shrugs causing our shoulders to bump

and heat to flare between us. "They're a bunch of college kids. I would imagine there isn't much that will keep them from making fools of themselves."

"You don't go to Hastings?"

He haunches down against the rain. Beads of it condense and fall into the springy hair of his beard and I find that I can't look away from the sight. My fingers itch to run through it and see if it is as soft as I imagine. "Nah, I graduated a long time ago, little girl. I manage our family business in town."

Brushing off the *little girl* I think of my family and how estranged we've become. "Must be nice to grow up here, have all of your friends and family be nearby."

At that he looks away, running a hand over his hair. He must have forgotten that he was wearing the beanie because he knocks it to the ground, revealing a full head of thick brown hair. He bends at the waist, the nearly see-through material of his shirt stretching across the broad expanse of his back to reveal outlines of even more ink.

For the first time, I think of using my gift for proactive reasons. I'd love to trace those lines and learn where he got them and why.

Or maybe I just want to see him with his shirt completely off.

Either way it doesn't matter because, for some reason, I can't read him at all. I don't know if I should feel relieved, concerned, or a little peeved, so I go for a combination of all three.

"They're all gone." He shoves the beanie back on his head. "My family, I mean. It's just me now."

His statement strikes a chord in me. Even surrounded by people, I felt completely alone. It makes me want to wrap my arm around this perfect stranger to let him know that he's not the only one.

"So if you don't go to Hastings, what were you doing creeping out in the middle of the woods at night?"

"I give tours, you know walk the trails with the tourists and talk about the local wildlife. Anyway, one of the people on today's tour left their bag in the woods. Didn't find it, but I came across you as I was heading back and wanted to make sure that you were okay."

I put my palm on his thigh and squeeze. Partly because I can't deny the urge to touch him and partly because I want to see if my lack of psychic response to him was a one-time thing. When I don't feel, hear or see anything after a few seconds, aside from the basic zing of attraction—which I can't deny either—I pull back. "I appreciate that, by the way."

"You're welcome, Sully," he says and I don't correct him. I like the way my name sounds coming out of his mouth. It sounds like sex and secrets, all gruff and forbidden. He opens his mouth and hesitates for a second before saying, "You want to get out of here? Maybe go to someplace a little less wet?"

I look back at the party, finally spotting my brother, who looks like he's having the time of his life. Telling him to take me home now would ruin his fun and I've already been a gigantic bitch about this move.

"I can't leave because I'm supposed to drive my brother back home later."

"We don't have to leave; my cabin is just over there." He nods towards the edge of the clearing where the party is taking place. "It's not much, but it'll keep you warm enough. I probably have some dry clothes you can use."

"I don't know; I wouldn't want to keep you—"

"It's not an obligation to talk to a beautiful woman, Sully. C'mon." He stands and offers his hand. The rain has slicked the material of his shirt to his skin and I can see every line of his defined pecs and abs, all one hundred of them. Dear God a part of me wants to be afraid of my visceral reaction to him. All the others are screaming for me to go with him.

He may as well be a stranger with candy leading me to his white van and I wouldn't care.

Ice colds drops of water find an opening at the back of his shirt and down my neck, making the decision an easy one. "Sure, anything to get out of the rain."

I take his hand again and shiver, though not from the cold. Being able to touch someone again without fear of what I may see is freeing and I find myself inching closer to him to revel in the feeling.

The sounds of the crowd filter through the night air, but it's more like background noise because the only thing I'm focused on is him. His house is one of the cabins dotting a back road on the edge of the forest. It must be nice to wake up with this kind of view every day.

I tug on his hand to get his attention. "This is your house?"

He looks down and pulls me closer, putting an arm around my shoulder to share his body heat. "Yeah, it's not much, but I like all of the space out here."

"Definitely better than being in the rain. Thanks, again."

"No problem. Want me to get you something to drink?"

I shrug out of his wet shirt and he takes it from me, throwing it in a pile on his dining room table. "Sure, anything would be great."

As he bangs around in the kitchen, I sit carefully on the edge of his well-worn sofa and study his house. The inside of the cabin isn't anything fancy. It's a sort of a studio-style open living space with the galley kitchen off to one side and the combination dining and living room to the other. It's decorated with a bunch of black and white nature images and several homey, handmade throws.

As he makes the drinks, I cross the living room to one of the pictures. It's a black and white study of a grove of trees. It could have been taken anywhere, but part of me already knows it was taken in the woods. Something tells me that he keeps this place near to his heart. I can totally understand that. I didn't want to leave my home either because it was the place that made me feel the closest to my parents. With my gift, I was able to grab memories from all over our house.

I didn't realize how much I missed that special kind of inconvenience until I touched the fridge at Nonna's and didn't get a vision of my dad grabbing a beer. Or when I started the coffee machine and didn't see my mom's sleepy morning face complete with hair sticking in every direction.

"Did you take these?" I ask, turning back to lean against the kitchen counter, suddenly curious about this mysterious gentle giant with the soulful brown eyes and predatory stare.

"No," Declan says, coming out of the bedroom already changed into a fresh pair of jeans and a T-shirt. "My dad was a photographer. These are all his."

"They're beautiful."

Declan comes to stand by my side. "Yeah, they are. I have tons of them at the shop in town. The tourists love them and I kinda like the thought of his work being out there in the world, you know? Some way for his memory to go on."

An image of my parents come to mind and I wonder how they'll be remembered. Both were business professionals and had little time for anything artistic. In fact, their memories are mostly confined to pictures and home videos.

"You're lucky to have that," I choke out, taking the mug from his hand. An image pops to mind as soon as my fingers graze the ceramic. I see Declan sitting behind the counter of what I assume is his shop.

Normally when I'm sucked into a vision I do everything I can to pull myself out, but this time, I find myself lingering, taking everything in. I want to know everything I can about this man and since I can't read him like everyone else, I'm reduced to second-hand snooping.

God, he looks lonely, is the first thing that comes to mind. He's sorting through inventory on the glass shop counter, the longer hair up on top pulled back into a little bun. Small wire-framed glasses are perched on his nose and he curses as they keep sliding down. He looks up with the coffee cup in hand and his eyes are drawn to the passersby outside of his front window. Families of three and four go by, not even looking at his door.

The shop is empty save for some serious dust motes in the air and I can tell not much has changed in the time since his father ran it. The wood paneling on the wall looks original and there are more of the black and white nature scenes as far back as I can see. Various tourist-y knick knacks cover the shelves and there are racks and racks of fishing and hunting gear that I don't even recognize. My parents weren't very outdoorsy. Tennis was about as far as my mom would go to working up a sweat.

The memory fades slowly, sweetly almost and I

blink rapidly trying to clear my head of the un-reality. Declan's fingers run through the hair at my nape, lifting the weight away from my neck and cupping my head with his large palm. And I forget everything but how close he is.

"Are you all right?" he asks, peering into my eyes.

I don't know if it's the atmosphere or the memory or the loneliness I felt from him that reminds me of my own, but I find myself leaning toward him. My hands lift up to rest on his broad shoulders and I get on my tip-toes to kiss his full lower lip.

The hand at the back of my head slides down my spine and rests on my hip. At first I think he may be trying to push me away. I make a sound in the back of my throat and take a half-step forward to bring our bodies flush together. In spite of the chill from my wet clothes, I can feel my body temperature rising. Whatever indecision he felt evaporates and his grip tightens.

I'd wondered what his facial hair would feel like. Would it tickle or chafe? Would I like it or love it? The jury is in and I may never kiss a man without any again. The soft bristle teases me on an entirely new level, causing gooseflesh to pepper my skin.

His lips are even softer than I imagined, especially in comparison with the rough scratch of his scruff. I could drown in the need for more. My senses are clogged with it, with him. The smokey-clean scent of his skin, the searing warmth of his palms slipping under my damp shirt.

He wasn't in my plans, but now I wonder if there wasn't a reason that I wound up in Hillsborough. Because a kiss this soul-shattering is anything but ordinary.

I make a sound of surprise when he moves back a few inches. My brows furrow and my stomach clenches. "I'm sorry, I didn't mean—"

Holy shit, what if he didn't want me to kiss him?

But he interrupts me by taking a few steps backwards and sitting on his couch. He tugs at my fingers and I walk towards him, the bit of apprehension returning because I know he's the type of man that can eat a girl like me right up.

"C'mere," he says, his voice gruff and I like it. I like that I did that to him, that I have that kind of effect on him. I like that he doesn't see me as weird or pitiful, he just sees me.

His hands guide me over his hips so that I'm straddling him. He pauses and his fingers trail up my hips and stomach, but what I enjoy more than that is the look of intense concentration on his face. When they reach my face, he cups my cheeks and brings my lips back down to his.

"You should probably leave," he says a few moments later, or maybe it's hours. I've completely lost track of everything but how he makes me feel.

I pull back, my arms still wrapped around his neck and my lips deliciously bruised. "What do you mean?"

He lays a kiss on the base of my throat, then kisses his way back up to my mouth. "Little girl like you. It's not safe to be here all alone."

I attempt a laugh, but it strangles on a moan when he nibbles at my ear. "I think I can take care of myself," I manage to say. I should be scared of him like I was of the creep, but I'm not. Maybe it's the fact that I can't read him, maybe it's because he kisses like a God. Whatever the reason, he doesn't scare me even though his words sound like a warning.

My phone vibrates on the couch where I set it and I groan, knowing that it must be my brother. I shoot Declan a wry smile. "That'll be my brother. Probably good timing, if I knew what time it was."

Even though it's the last thing I want to do, I get back to my feet.

"Let me get some jackets and an umbrella. I'll walk you back."

The more time passes while he's gone, the more I wonder what makes him different. I've never had my gift falter, not once since my parents died.

My phone buzzes again and I frown, shooting Sam a text that I'm on my way. Declan returns with everything in hand. I look back at my phone to Sam telling me to hurry up because he's cold.

"That's him again, apparently alcohol and women aren't enough to distract him from the fact that it's freezing cold and wet out there."

"Better get you back then." He holds the jacket up and I shrug into it, nuzzling the collar to commit his scent to memory when he isn't looking. For once, I wish I could use my gift on someone, at least to know what he's thinking.

The rain has slowed to a sprinkle and the lights in the clearing have dimmed considerably. I follow Declan's lead and wonder what the right words are after an encounter like this. We make it back to the crowd before I come up with anything.

Sam notices me from across the way and waves. I lift a hand in response and turn back to Declan, who is standing at the edge of the tree line. "That's my brother," I say lamely.

"I see that," he says, a smile curling underneath his beard.

"Anyway, I'd like to see you again." I cough, and know my face must be going red. I don't know how old he is, older than me for sure, but definitely old enough to get hit on by women much more smooth and confident than I am. "I mean if you want," I finish lamely.

I couldn't have been more ridiculous if I tried.

He hesitates and I wonder if maybe I read him wrong. Sure kissing a stranger may be normal to him. Hell, he probably flirts with tourists all the time. All I know is I want to see him again.

I want to find out why my gift doesn't work on him.

Even more, I want to kiss him again.

"You don't want to see me again," he says.

"Why not?" I ask. Immediately I know without a doubt I do want to see him again. Apple and Eve and all that. Forbidden fruit.

"Probably not a good idea. I shouldn't have kissed you in the first place."

"*I* kissed *you*," I say, my tone indignant.

At this, his lips curve a little, but they only make me frown in response. "I'm not the kind of man you should be getting involved with little girl."

"Don't call me that. And like I said. I know how to take care of myself. I can handle you."

"I guess we'll see about that. Give me your phone."

I unlock it and hand it over. I think he's programming his number in. When he hands it back, I check the screen. I see he's texted himself. Before I can say anything, I get another text with a time.

When I look up, he's melting into the crowd.

"See you tomorrow!" I holler at his back, but I'm smiling.

Chapter Three
Sully

My bedroom looks like all of my moving boxes have exploded. Nonna walked in a few minutes ago, took a look around, and then walked back out. I tried on everything I owned, but I was having one of those days where nothing fit or looked right. I finally decide on a pair of jeans and a cute but simple top which made my brown eyes pop. For the first time in a while, I take some time putting on makeup and doing my hair, even though it's entirely possible Declan's idea of a date may involve trekking through the great outdoors and my efforts may be ruined.

If this is even a date at all. Whatever. There's nothing wrong with putting in a little effort. Especially if I can facilitate another one of those kisses. What harm could come from a little kiss?

I'm putting the finishing touches on with a swipe of mascara and a touch of gloss when Nonna appears in the doorway. Her eyes carefully avoid the piles of wrinkled laundry and the mangled boxes piled three deep. "Have plans tonight?"

"Actually, yes. I hope you don't mind if I skip dinner." I glance at her as I put away my makeup. Her hair is thinner and a lighter brown than my mom's was, but they both share the same soft, round face and petite build.

She leans against the doorframe. "Of course not. I want you to feel at home here. I'm glad you are making friends so quickly. You remind me of Rebecca in that way. She never met a soul who wasn't her instant best friend."

I find myself smiling. "I wouldn't say I'm that friendly. I think Sam inherited that gene."

Her eyes twinkle. "Then it must be a boy." I start to object to her use of the word *boy*, but she holds up her hands. "Don't worry, I'm not going to pry. There are good people here. I know Hastings isn't exactly what you planned, but I hope you'll find this place to be your home, too."

"I know, Nonna. And you know how much we

appreciate it." I look away, double checking the contents of my purse so I can choke back the sting of tears.

"Of course, *bambina*. That doesn't make it any easier." There's a pause of silence and I wonder if she's remembering Mom, too. I've been so lost in my own grief that I hadn't even paused to consider what it's been like for Nonna to lose her only daughter.

I put down the purse and cross the room to stand in front of her. There is no sign of tears, but Nonna's never been one to cry. Like my mom, she's made of stronger stuff. But I can still see the haunted look on her face like I'm looking at my own. I pull her into my arms for a hug. It takes her a second to respond, but I feel her small arms come around me and am enveloped by the scent of her sandalwood perfume.

A few seconds later, I feel another pair of arms wrap around me and I hear Sam's voice say, "Group hug!"

He squeezes tightly, compressing my lungs, and I choke out, "Sam, oh my God! Let go before you squish us to death."

"What's with the family reunion?" he asks, throwing an arm around Nonna's shoulders.

"Noth—"

"Sullivan has a date," Nonna says, eyes shining.

I groan and slip my purse strap over my shoulder. "Reunion over. I have to get going or I'm going to be late."

Taking advantage of Sam's slack-jawed shock, I slip by the two of them and bound down the stairs. I almost make it out of the front door when Sam catches me by the arm.

"What do you mean you're going on a date?" he demands.

"I don't know if I would call it a date," I hedge. A hookup? What would Declan call this?

"Is there a dude involved?"

I bite my lip. "Yes."

"Did he ask you out?" he asks.

"No," I say triumphantly. "I asked him out."

"Then it's a date," he states. His eyebrows pull inward and he frowns. "You don't talk to me the entire way from Florida to Indiana, but you can go on a date with some guy you don't even know."

"Sam—" I start, but he cuts me off.

"No, I get it, *Sullivan*. You want me to get lost. I can do that. It's not like when we were kids and would have sleepovers on the living room floor and talk 'til dawn. You're all grown up now. You have no parents, so you might as well push away your brother, too. Why not be completely alone? Just makes it easier."

My heart thuds dully in my ears and a tear streaks down my cheek. "Are you kidding me? I went out with you last night."

He smiles, but it's empty and that sends a shock through my heart and I worry that maybe my bad treatment has gone too far for repair. "No, I get it now, Sul. Go. Enjoy your date."

Before I can come up with a response, he turns on his heel and stalks toward the kitchen and out of sight. I stand, numb, in the foyer until my phone vibrates in my back pocket. I glance down at it and find a text.

Hey, this is Declan.

I look up one more time to see if maybe Sam has come back, but the downstairs is empty.

He is right. I am alone.

Not knowing what to do or what to say to mend that bridge, I leave, locking the door behind me.

The GPS takes me to what looks like the parking lot for a couple of abandoned buildings. *Well, this is off to a good start.* I double check that I put the address in correctly, but it still tells me that I've reached my destination. The concrete is glistening with the leftovers of a storm and puddles of water reflect the lights from the buildings. If I squint, it almost feels a little romantic. Kind of like a slasher film, but what can you do?

Headlights flash over the parking lot and Declan brings his truck to a stop beside mine. I can't see through the tint which makes the butterflies in my stomach go crazy. God, it's been a long time since I've felt this way. My hands are clammy and my throat is dry. If I'm not careful, this feeling is going to get completely out of control. Maybe this wasn't such a good idea.

A few sharp raps against my window make me jump in my seat. Declan bends down and grins at me. I manage to keep my heart from jumping out of my chest. Barely.

When I unlock the doors, he tugs the handle and leans down in the open space. "I'm glad you found it okay."

"Wherever 'it' is." I peer back at the nondescript

faces of the brick buildings behind me. "Care to tell me what we're doing?"

"Where's the fun in that?" He offers me a hand and I take it. He helps me out and neither of us let go when I'm up on my feet. I shut the door with my hip as he leads me toward one of the buildings. "You're going to get the official Hillsborough welcome tour. The dry version."

"C'mon," I say and I'm mortified to find that my voice is breathy with excitement. "Where are you taking me?"

Declan flashes me a grin. "Now what kind of surprise would that be?"

"The kind that doesn't feel like an episode of *Criminal Minds*."

He laughs at that and says, "You have an overactive imagination."

"Says the man leading me into an abandoned building."

"You're going to eat your words in a few minutes."

"I hope you mean figuratively."

The door to the building is old and doesn't look like it's been painted in my lifetime. Declan raises his free hand to knock and I'm struck by the fact that I'm still holding onto the other one. His hand is warm around mine and I can't help but notice how well they fit together. When I look up I catch him staring at me, there's a warm glow reflecting back in his eyes.

The space between us heats and I wonder if he's going to flip tradition and kiss me at the beginning of the date instead of the end. Thoughts of the night before make me hope it's the former. I'm about to do something completely out of character—again—and make the first move, when the door opens to reveal a middle-aged man with neatly trimmed facial hair and a hefty gut. He motions us in, slapping Declan on the back.

"Good to see you again, Mr. Cain. And you brought a lovely lady with you today." He turns to me and takes my free hand, bringing it to his lips. "*Bellisima*, you must be Sullivan. Welcome, I am Antonio. Come, come, I have a table ready for you."

I follow Declan down a dimly lit hallway which opens up into a dining room full of mismatched tables with red tablecloths and low lighting. Soft candlelight flickers from tea lights floating in water in the centerpieces. Antonio leads us to a table in the corner and pulls out a chair for me. I reluctantly let go of Declan's hand to sit. Antonio provides a menu as Declan takes the seat opposite of me.

"Thank you," I say to Antonio.

"*Prego.* Can I start you off with anything to drink?"

"A beer, please, Tony," Declan says.

"Soda is fine, thank you." Antonio smiles widely and winks at me before departing.

"Terrifying, isn't it?" Declan says.

I blush. "Well, what's a girl to think when you take her to an empty parking lot in the middle of nowhere?"

"You say that like we didn't meet in the middle of the woods."

"Point taken. You didn't bring me back there so I guess that's a good thing," I tell him as I flip through the pages of the menu. I immediately decide on the soup and salad. When Declan doesn't respond I glance up and say, "What?" when I find him looking at me again.

He shakes his head ruefully. "Nothing, I'm just wondering what you're doing with a man like me."

"A man like you?" Does he mean older?

But Antonio interrupts to ask for our orders before Declan can respond. He brings out garlic bread and marinara sauce along with our drinks. I dive in, breaking the bread into pieces and dipping them into the sauce.

"I never would have known this place was here," I tell him.

"Hillsborough's best kept secret. Only the locals know it's here and we keep it from the tourists."

"So you've lived here your whole life?"

"Pretty much," he says with a nod before taking a pull from his beer. "I can't imagine living anywhere else."

"You've never wanted to go to the city? See what that's like?" I wonder if he ever gets out of his office or if every day is like that for him. It was like he was letting the world and his life pass him by. At least I have Sam to annoy and keep me company. I suppose now I can add Nonna to that list as well.

Declan doesn't have anyone.

"No, never. I like my space, remember?" he says and clears his throat. "So, what brings you to the wilds of Indiana?"

"My parents were killed in a car accident last year. My grandmother lives here and smoothed the way for my brother and me to attend Hastings-Albrect."

Declan reaches across the table and takes my hand. I'm going to need to be careful or holding his hand is going to become my new favorite thing. "I'm sorry to hear that, Sullivan."

I offer him a wobbly smile. "Thanks. It gets a little easier every day."

"Time helps, I imagine. And dinners with your newest friend."

This time, my smile is genuine. "Definitely."

Though I'm hoping to convince him to be more than friends.

"Now where are you taking me?"

I haven't been on very many dates and none of them had ever impressed me as much as the little Italian restaurant that Declan took me to. After Antonio brought us our food, we spent the next two hours talking about *everything*. I can't remember the last time I ever felt so comfortable with another person. It doesn't hurt that he makes my body hum with the simplest of touches.

We finished our meal and Antonio cleared away the plates and brought us cheesecake. As we nibbled on the decadent dessert, strains of music floated over the air as Antonio sat at a piano in the corner and began to serenade us in Italian. Needless to say by the time dinner was over, I practically floated out of the restaurant. Declan led me to his truck with the promise that the night was only just beginning.

"To my place," he says, flipping on the turn signal.

"Um, your place?" I ask. "Confident, aren't you?"

He flashes me a smile and pauses at a deserted stop sign to cup my cheek with his free hand. "Much as that intrigues me, it's not what you think."

"Really?" I scoot over to his side and fit my body against his. After the past two hours, I need to put my hands on him or I'm going to burst into flames.

He accepts my kiss at the next stoplight. "I can't wait to get my hands on you either."

By the time we get to his house, I'm fidgeting in my seat, and rubbing my thighs together to stave off the ache. I can't quite seem to keep my hands to myself. They trace the lines of ink on his forearms and squeeze his knee.

He helps me out of the truck and my body slides down his before my feet touch the ground. We seem to have used up all of our words during dinner because I can't focus on anything other than his lips.

Declan moves closer, pressing me against the side of his truck. I bring my hands up to his shoulders and my head falls back. The hands at my waist bring our bodies together. At the first brush of his lips, I gasp and then his mouth covers mine and my mind goes completely, blissfully blank.

The kiss isn't wild or overwhelming. It's just the light brush of his lips against mine, but nothing—nothing—has ever felt so good. He brings one hand up to push back the hair from my face and I find myself leaning into his touch. When the hand on my hip pulls me more fully against him, I go weak at the knees.

When we part, I can't seem to catch my breath. If it weren't for the solidity of the truck behind my back, I very well could have sank into a puddle at his feet.

"Wow," I murmur without thinking.

Declan nips at my lips again and my eyes flutter closed. He steps back, breaking the kiss, and cool air comes between us. "I'll take that as a compliment."

I blush. "Or you could forget that I said it completely."

"Not a chance, beautiful. C'mon, I've got something else to show you."

After that soul-shattering kiss, I will pretty much follow him anywhere. He takes my hand and leads me past his cabin and shed to a trail in his backyard which leads into the woods. Visibility is essentially nonexistent so I grasp his hand more tightly.

"You're sure this is okay?" I ask.

"Absolutely. If it makes you feel any better, I know these woods like the back of my hand. I promise I'll keep you safe."

"My life is in your hands, so I'm going to hold you to that."

He stops and presses another kiss to my lips. "Feel free to hold me anytime."

The trees suddenly stop and a clearing appears before us. There's an old abandoned building in the center of the clearing and a blanket laid on the grassy floor a few feet away.

"What's this?"

He tugs my hand. "Best view in the world," he says. He sits on the blanket and pulls me down next to him. Declan arranges my body in the crook of his arm. He gestures above us. "See?"

I look up and gasp. "It's beautiful."

"I told you." The tips of his fingers trace the line of my arm. "This is the old tourist center. It's pretty much abandoned now, but I come out here some-times when I need to be alone. It's kind of like my special place."

"And you brought me here."

He looks down and the corner of his lips quirk up a little. "Maybe I think you're special, too."

I'd heard of romance before. I'd seen it every day with my parents. I just never thought I'd find anything like it in my lifetime. If this were a couple hundred years ago I would have swooned.

Instead, I slide up so I'm propped on my arms above him. His amber eyes are bright even in the darkness. One arm is thrown up, his head leaning against it in a casual pose. I'd studied him throughout dinner, but my eyes can't get enough of his square jaw and full lips.

I shift, moving over him until my mouth is even with his. I'm pleased to find that he's lost that smile, his eyes now focused on my lips. When I lean down, his hand cups my cheek to guide my face down to his.

As our lips touch, I shiver again, before a loud snap comes from somewhere in the woods and I jump up, bumping noses with him along the way.

"Ouch, shit!"

"Smooth," he says, holding his nose.

I shove his shoulder with my free hand. "Jerk." The trees around us are silent now, but the mood is broken. "Are you sure there isn't anything just out there lying in wait, getting ready to make us dinner?"

"What, like a group of hungry frat guys?" he

teases. "I'm pretty sure you'll be able to protect me if that ends up being the case."

Even though he jokes, the hairs on the back of my neck stand on end. I scan the trees, but I don't see anything. Determined to enjoy tonight, I relax beside him, tangling our legs together. "I'll keep you safe," I tell him.

A grunt of agreement leaves his mouth before he takes my lips for a slow, sweet kiss, my head propped on the crook of his arm. By the end, his body is hovering over mine and I've never felt so safe and cherished. He starts to slide down, his bulk folding up to accommodate the movement. Heat washes over me and I suck in a deep breath, the anticipation sharp and sweet.

He lifts the bottom of my T-shirt with his nose and slides it slowly up my stomach. His eyes catch mine and he pauses, waiting for my reaction. When I do nothing other than lift up on my elbows to watch, he smiles and shifts his weight onto one hand and uses the other to draw my shirt up to just underneath my breasts.

"Do you want me to stop?" he asks tentatively.

"I want you, please," I manage.

What I wouldn't give to know what he's thinking right now. To know if he's feeling as into me as I am into him. He presses his lips against the soft skin of my hip and my breathing shallows as I wonder exactly where he'll kiss next.

When his eyes flick up to catch mine, I stop breathing entirely. He nuzzles his way up until he reaches the barrier of my shirt. My fingers tremble, but I grip my shirt and tug it up and over my head. I don't know if it's the darkness or the light from the moon, but his eyes seem to glow a soft gold when I look back at him.

I lay back flat on the blanket as he crawls over me, my hands going up to grip his shoulders. His soft lips trace patterns on my stomach, pausing to nip and entice. His deft fingers pull down the cups of my bra and my nipples tighten and ache in the cool night air. I arch my neck as he takes one breast into his big hand and the other he covers with his mouth.

I groan into the night and bring my legs up to capture his hips, needing him, all of him. Soft flicks of his tongue and gentle tweaks from his fingers leave me boneless beneath his hot, hard body.

When I'm writhing beneath him, nearly mind-less from it all, the hand on my breast begins the slow, torturous journey to the waistband of my jeans. I suck in a breath as his fingers release the buttons from its catch and draw the zipper down one tooth at a time. His fingers get caught in the confines of the tight material and I shimmy them partway down my hips. Freed, he traces the lines of my panties, finding me wet and needy for him.

"You need this don't you?" he murmurs, his breath skimming over my already sensitive nipple. "You want me to touch you here? Make you come out here where anyone can see us?"

Oh God, I shouldn't want that, hadn't even considered the possibility, but once he mentions it, my hips buck underneath him. Needing a focus in the maelstrom of sensation, I pull his lips back down to mine and kiss him with abandon—wild and hungry.

His fingers slip into my panties, making me whimper into his mouth. They dip down and cover me, one finger tracing my lips with aching slowness. It dips in, finding me slick and wet with need. I go still at the sensation of having him inside of me. His free arm slides beneath me to cradle my head and enfold me completely in his warm embrace.

The little grunts he's making in my ear coupled with the masterful efforts of his fingers cause my body to tighten all over. Fingers now slick from me find my clit and fling me higher with a few quick movements. He finds a rhythm, one that makes my hips jerk in time against him and he keeps it up, murmuring encouraging filthy words in my ear, until I break apart against him.

He kisses me as I come down, my body shaking from the remnants of pleasure. I open my eyes and find his gold ones looking back at me, a satisfied smile curls around his lips.

"Think you needed that," Declan says, his voice gruff.

"I think I needed you," I reply without thinking.

He drops his head to the curve of my neck. "Watching you like that was the hottest thing I've ever seen. Please tell me you don't have anything to do tomorrow because I need to do that again as soon as possible."

I blush in the darkness, my smile so wide that my cheeks ache with the effort. "Oh God, I knew there was a reason why I shouldn't have signed up for morning classes."

He groans against my throat. "You're killing me," he says.

I tug on his hair until I can see his face. "But I can meet you after. We can go to a movie or something."

"My afternoon is packed with tours, but you can tag along."

He helps me straighten my clothes and get to my feet. My body still thrums with the aftershocks from the orgasm, so I don't process what he means until we start to head back to his truck.

"Wait do you mean like fishing or something?"

He quirks a brow at me. "Yeah, out on the river. What, you've never been fishing before?"

"Does gaming count?" I ask hopefully.

He laughs. "No, I don't think so. C'mon you'll enjoy it. After we can grab something to eat, maybe come back here for a movie."

I forget about the fishing and remember his hands the entire drive back to the warehouse where my truck waits in the parking lot. Somehow along the way I find myself agreeing. As he pulls to a stop, a hollow feeling takes up residence in my stomach at the realization that the night is ending.

He pins me against my door for another bone-melting kiss and when it's over, my hands are gripping his biceps and I'm breathing heavily.

"Can't wait to see you tomorrow," he says, his lips brushing against mine.

I get into my truck and watch him from my rearview as I drive way.

Maybe things are finally starting to turn around.

Chapter Four
Sully

You know a date has gone well when you find yourself waking up the next morning with the kind of smile that doesn't go away, even when faced with the likes of Sam before he's had a cup of coffee. And I thought I was bad without caffeine.

Flashes of the night before make my lips curl and my face flush warm. The curve of my neck itches from the resulting beard burn. Those moments with Declan when I can forget the tragedy of my own life are worth everything. No psychic white noise, no pressure from my brother or expectations from my grandmother. I couldn't have dreamt a better night.

With those thoughts on my mind, I pour myself a bowl of cereal and ignore Sam's scowl from the other side of the breakfast bar. Last night was too perfect to let him ruin it.

"You excited to start classes today?" I ask around a bite.

"Over-freaking-joyed," he mumbles, glaring at the sunlight streaming in through the kitchen windows.

With no end to his attitude in sight, I finish my cereal and dump the bowl in the sink. I start to leave, swinging my messenger bag over my shoulder, but stop at the door. I turn to Sam with thoughts of all the first days of school we've shared in the past. His scowl is now directed at his coffee instead of me.

"Have a good day today, Sam." He looks up in surprise, but I leave before he can say anything else.

Nonna is letting him borrow her car for the day, so I have the truck to myself. I reach a hand in my bag for my phone but come up empty. I curse and dump out its contents but have no luck.

"Shit," I murmur. I had it in my pocket last night while we were in the woods because I remember checking the time when we started to leave. "Shit, shit, shit." I must have dropped it.

I check the time on the dash clock and find that I have just enough time to swing around Declan's cabin to grab it before class. Hopefully the ground didn't get too wet overnight. The last thing I need is to fork out the cash for a replacement phone.

It must be the residual dregs from the date, but I find myself smiling as I make the drive through Hillsborough to Declan's cabin. The sun's barely up when I get there, but I can tell by the lack of cars in the drive that he's already gone to work. God, it's only been a couple of hours, but I'm already excited just to see him again.

The woods look completely different in the daylight. They've lost a little bit of their magic. I wrap my arms around my waist to stave off the early morning chill. Without the big, reassuring presence of Declan by my side, the trees have a decidedly creepy quality. I laugh at myself as I pick my way through the trail, even though I may be walking a little bit faster.

I search the grass and plants for the glint of my phone but still don't see anything. A stray root catches my ankle, bringing me down with a strangled scream. The hard impact with the musty earth knocks the air right out of my lungs. Dew-slick vegetation coats my legs. Fantastic. I am definitely going to be late for class, which is not the impression I want to make.

I roll over to my stomach, my hands sliding on

the wet ground as I get back to my feet. I start to wipe them on my shorts, but realize it isn't dew, but thick, red blood. The memory slams into me like a Mack truck.

Heavy breathing fills my ears and a strangled scream fills my chest. I'm lost, running through the woods without an end in sight. I twist my ankle, but I keep running because whatever is behind me is going to kill me if I stop. Branches catch on my clothes and I lose one shoe along the way, but I don't stop, I can't.

A terrifying high-pitched scream comes from all directions, sending ice through my chest. I sob, my head twisting wildly to find a break in the trees, but they're endless. The scream comes again, but this time it sounds closer, like it's right behind me. I'm so worried that it's *right there* that I don't see the limb crossing my path and I come down, slamming into the ground.

I turn over with a groan, the wind knocked out of me, when I hear a twig snap.

I come back to reality with that sound echoing through my ears.

My gaze spins wildly and lands on the body of a young woman, her foot jutting out onto the trail, the lip of her sandals dangling from a single toe. I stumble back and slip on the bloody foliage again, but manage to keep my footing by grabbing hold of a branch.

The leaves shift with the wind, giving me a clear view of the mutilated body. An arm obstructs what is left of her face and her bare body is stained red. It pools around her and splatters across leaves. A river of it flows across the trail. Thick ragged slashes pucker across her stomach, legs, and even across the skin of her pearl-white breasts. There are entire chunks of her flesh missing, likely from animals that had come for a midnight snack.

Her other hand stretches out to the side, open, beckoning.

I choke on my sobbing breaths as I fumble on my unsteady feet. I make my way back to Declan's house blindly, but the image of the body stays burned into the back of my eyelids.

I throw up in the bushes before I ever make it out of the woods. A sour taste lingers and my vision flashes white as I yank open the door to my truck. I stumble trying to get into the cab and lean my head against the cool leather to catch my breath.

What kind of small town is this?

Chapter Five
Sully

The sheriff's station isn't quite what I'd expect, though by the looks on the faces of the deputies, they didn't quite expect me either. I stumble through the glass door, smearing blood over the department logo.

The fluorescent lights are dull and one of them flickers drunkenly in the corner. Ratty old chairs and a couple of tables like the ones you'd find in an old doctor's waiting room fill the space. There's even a glass partition with an older lady sitting behind it. I stagger across the room, knocking my shin on one of the chairs and slapping my hands down on the slice of blue paneled countertop.

The lady behind the glass partition doesn't look

up until she finishes whatever she's writing on the clipboard in front of her. Her name tag reads Debbie. When she does, her eyes catch on my blood-stained hands and widen.

"My god, are you okay?" she asks, standing.

"Someone's...hurt. In the woods. Someone needs to go help her," I babble.

Debbie disappears behind the wall and then the only other door in the room opens and she beckons me forward. "Are you hurt?"

I shake my head. "I'm fine." I look down at my hands numbly. "It's not my blood."

Debbie leads me into an empty conference room of sorts. She guides me to an old, worn black office chair and I sit down before the strength completely leaks from my legs.

"Did you hurt someone?" she asks carefully.

"No, I just found her." Tears sting my nose. "I don't think there was anything I could do. She didn't...she was dead." My voice breaks and I look away, studying the dust-glazed fern in the corner.

"Can you tell me where she is, so I can send someone over?"

"Um, I'm not sure exactly, but it was behind Declan Cain's cabin. There's a trail behind his house that leads into the forest."

She grabs one of those little pointy cups from the water cooler and brings it to me. I cup it with both hands, frowning at how they bloody up the white paper.

"I'll be right back," she says. "I'll bring you something to clean up with."

I don't know how long she's gone. When she comes back the water has gone warm in the cup and I haven't been able to choke any down, no matter how disgusting and dry my mouth feels.

"A couple of deputies are on their way out to Mr. Cain's place. Why don't you take your time? You can tell me what happened when you're ready."

I take a deep breath and manage to sip some of the water before launching into my story of the past hour. Debbie doesn't visibly react; she just takes notes on one of those yellow legal pads with a careful hand. When I'm done, she takes samples of the blood on my hands and scrapes some of it from my fingernails. She gets a copy of my I.D. and then, finally, allows me to wash off the blood from my hands and arms with wet paper towels.

"Is there anyone I can call to bring you a change of clothes? I'm afraid it may be a while, and we're going to need those for evidence."

Nodding, I say, "My grandmother. Suzanna Thomas."

"Why don't you give me her number and I'll give her a call for you?"

Debbie rises to leave and I stop her with a hand on her arm. "Did they find her? Was she dead?"

"Yes, they did, Ms. Thomas. She was."

After Debbie leaves my stomach pitches and I heave into the trashcan, but there's nothing left to throw up. I wet one of the leftover paper towels with water from the water cooler and press it against the fevered flesh of my forehead.

A few minutes later Debbie comes back, this time with Nonna on her heels. Nonna's face is sheet-white, as are the knuckles around a plastic bag full of clothes.

"Oh my God, Sullivan." She rushes inside, but Debbie stops her before she can throw her hands around me.

"Ma'am. If you'll give her the change of clothes, she can go to the bathroom and change."

Nonna's face is pained, but she nods, her lips pressing together.

Debbie instructs me on taking off and storing each piece of clothing. I should be embarrassed getting naked in front of this stranger, but I'm not. The only thing on my mind is the image of that girl's mangled body. Everything else pales in comparison. Once that's taken care of, I scrub the rest of my skin furiously with harsh hand soap from the dispenser and the rough brown paper towels feel like sandpaper. When I'm done—my skin an angry shade of red —I still don't quite feel clean enough.

I'm not sure if I ever will again.

Nonna envelopes me in her arms the second I leave the bathroom and I'm too tired to protest. My arms go around her and we stand there for a few minutes until Debbie comes back for a few more questions. For the first time, I don't try to escape the transference of feelings and memories. Warmth and worry emanate from Nonna and provide me with a much needed moment of strength.

The yellow legal pad is back and I watch as her pen scratches across its surface. "What were you doing in the woods?" Debbie asks.

"Looking for my phone. I was on my way to class and didn't want to leave it in the woods in case it got wet."

"So you'd been to the area before this morning."

"Yes," I say, resting my head on my palms

because I don't want to see the look on Nonna's face as I relate my story. "I was on a date last night and he took me into the woods. We looked at the stars...We weren't even out there for that long because I have... had an early class this morning."

"Around what time would you say you were in the woods?"

"Maybe nine or so. We went to dinner around seven and stayed for a couple hours before he took me there."

"May I have his name, please?"

"Declan. Declan Cain. His cabin is the one I was telling you about." Finally, it clicks in my brain why she's asking. "You don't think he...that he's the one that did this, do you?" My stomach heaves again, but I manage to control it. Barely. I thought I knew Declan, even though we'd only seen each other a couple of times. My gift should have taught me that what lies beneath the surface is a different story compared to the airs people put on. But still, a part of me knows he could never do something like this.

"We're just getting the facts, Ms. Thomas."

When I glance at Nonna, she's staring at me open-mouthed. My brows furrow. When I catch her gaze she shakes her head. Confused and with a headache brewing, I turn back to the deputy and finish the interview.

Numb to my bones, I lay my head against the conference table when Debbie leaves again after her last question. As we wait, I wonder what the hell is going on.

Chapter Six
Declan

I'm used to the whispers that follow me around town. I'm used to the seclusion and loneliness. I expect those things.

What I didn't expect was Sully.

The bell rings signaling another customer. I pause my inventory on a shipment of new reels and glance up. "Afternoon," I greet one of the county deputies. "Can I help you?"

"Declan Cain?" he asks without returning my greeting. When he doesn't look around and doesn't answer my question, my hackles start to rise.

"That's me. What can I do for you?" I try to keep my voice steady, but I can't say the same for my heartbeat. Something feels off.

"We're going to need to talk to you for a minute,

sir. Do you mind coming over to the courthouse with us?" Over his shoulder I can see a police car with another deputy leaning against the hood.

"What is this about?" I ask as I wipe my hands on a cloth.

"There's been a murder near your property, and we have a few questions considering the location and your history."

I heave a sigh. I knew something like this was going to happen. I just wish it didn't have to happen now that I've met Sullivan. Now that I've convinced myself it may just be okay to have her. To keep her. The secrets I keep were bound to get out sooner or later, I just wish it was later.

"Let me tell my guy that I'll be out, okay?"

"Five minutes."

I scrub a hand over my beard. This is going to dredge up so many things I'd hoped to keep buried. Things I am not ready to deal with or talk about. Things I don't want Sullivan to know. At least not yet.

There's no need to go searching for Red. I find him standing in the hallway with a menacing look on his face. He's worked with me since my Dad died and has been a friend of the family for as long as I can remember.

"What the hell do they want?" he asks, crossing his arms over his chest.

"They just have a couple of questions. I'm not sure exactly what happened, but I need to go with them for a while. Can you watch over the shop until I get back?"

"You don't even have to ask. I'll see you when I see you."

"I'll let you know if I'm going to be so late that you'll need to close up."

"Don't worry, I'll be here if you need anything."

"Thanks, Red."

Red claps a hand on my back and I turn to go with the deputies.

The sheriff's office is already a circus which is my first clue that shit has hit the proverbial fan. I spot Sullivan huddled in the corner with Suzanna Thomas and that's the second clue. Then, I come to a realization that has me staggering. Suzanna must be the grandmother who Sullivan spoke about, which is just my fucking luck.

The deputies lead me into the station. Sullivan

hears the door slam behind us and looks up at me. Shame washes over me like a bucket of cold water and I avert my eyes.

They lead me to a conference room and settle around me, their voices low as they whisper to each other. When they're all seated at the table, the Chief of Police T.J. Rickman, a man I'd known my whole life, sits in front of me, his elbows braced on his knees.

"Hey, Dec, I'm sorry to pull you out of work like this."

I drag a hand through my hair. "No, T.J., I understand. I want to help in any way I can."

"We appreciate that, and we'll get through this as fast as we can."

"They didn't tell me exactly what happened."

T.J. sighs and his gaze drops to the floor. "Your girl, Sullivan? She came across a body in the woods behind your place. Looked like it had been mauled or something."

Furious and sick to my stomach that she'd been there, alone, I rock back in my chair. "I've been at the shop since six this morning. We had a couple of early trips planned."

T.J. nods. "And last night?"

I tell him about my date with Sullivan, regret

once again rising up like bile in my stomach. "I was at my place, alone, by ten until I left for work this morning."

"According to the M.E. she was killed around seven in another location and then dumped behind your place. Ms. Thomas confirmed your alibi so we aren't holding you or charging you for anything. Just trying to get all the facts."

"Are you interviewing all the residents with cabins in the area, or just me?" The question gnaws at my stomach.

"Considering what happened to your father and the similarities between that case and this one we had to be sure."

That's what I was afraid of. "I understand, T.J. Like I said, I want to do whatever I can to help. Do you need anything else?"

"That's it for now, but just stay close in case we have any more questions."

"Of course." I get to my feet and accept T.J.'s hand for a quick shake.

The interview, surprisingly, is the easiest part. What I'm dreading is waiting in the lobby. I take a step forward and she immediately comes to my side, wrapping her arms around my waist like I hadn't just been brought in for questioning about a vicious murder.

"I'm so glad you're here," she says into the material of my shirt. "I knew you couldn't have anything to do with it, but they wouldn't let me call you and I still haven't found my cell phone. Are you okay? What did they do?"

Carefully, I disentangle her arms and put a careful distance between us. I offer her an uneasy smile. "I'm sorry to put you through this, Sullivan. It won't happen again."

Her dark ponytail has snarls in it and the shirt she's wearing is wrinkled. There's a faint red stain on the curve of her neck and my eyes latch onto it. She brings a hand to the spot, rubbing it self-consciously.

"I'm sorry," she whispers. "They haven't let me leave yet and there was b-blood everywhere."

I squeeze my eyes closed in an attempt to control my temper. "You don't have anything to apologize for. This was not your fault."

"I was so scared."

"You won't have to be scared again," I tell her. Suzanna Thomas clears her throat behind Sullivan, her pantsuit is flawless and there isn't a hair out of place. She was like that on the night we first met, too. I take her hint and put more distance between us.

Sullivan's brows crease. "What are you doing?"

"I meant what I said, Sully. I don't think it's a good idea for us to see each other again."

She brings her eyes to mine, staring up at me in confusion. "I don't understand."

Even though Suzanna's mouth pinches, I lean forward and press a kiss to Sully's brow. "Ask your grandmother."

Sully glances back and forth between us as I straighten and move away from her. "What does she have to do with anything?"

"I'm sorry," I say again. "Take care."

Then I leave without looking back.

Chapter Seven
Sully

A few days later, I still haven't forgiven Nonna for not answering any of my burning questions. She hasn't said a word about the matter since we left the police station. Once Sam learned about the whole ordeal he hasn't done anything but hover around me. At home, in between classes at school. No matter how many scathing words I fling at him, I can't seem to shake his new found hobby of shadowing me.

I grab a jug of orange juice from the fridge and bump into Sam who was standing behind me. I screech and whirl around. "That's it. I'm done with this, Sam. I've told you a million times that I don't need you to follow me around."

"A girl was murdered, Sully." He holds up a

hand when I open my mouth to object to his use of my nickname. "I'll damn well follow you if I have to put a tracking device under your skin."

"Don't be morbid. The people at the Chronicle are saying it was just an animal attack."

"That's because the cops don't have any other leads. Until they find the human or animal responsible, you're just going to have to live with your new bodyguard."

I groan and put the orange juice away after pouring myself a glass. "Fine, but can you keep at least a ten-foot distance between us? I'm tired of your girlfriend wannabes thinking I'm some sort of competition."

"Fine," he says. "As long as you keep your distance from that guy."

"That guy didn't do anything wrong that I'm aware of. In fact, he was perfectly respectful, not that I owe you any explanation."

"The hell you don't."

"If anyone deserves an explanation, it's me. Yet Nonna doesn't seem to think any of my questions deserve answers."

"I don't care who he is. He's obviously a danger to you and you need to stay away from him."

I roll my eyes at him and pack up my bag for my

second day of doing work-study at the Hillsborough Chronicle. The university offers a program for students to shadow during the summer as an extra credit. With none of my other classes available and no positions open at any of the law firms, the Chronicle was my last resort. When the managing editor learned that I discovered the body in Swift River, he couldn't wait to grill me for all the details and take me under his wing. That lasted for a couple hours until he tired of me. Then he left me to fact check and do grunt work for the real reporters.

Thankfully Sam leaves for an early class so I won't have to put up with him hovering. For a while at least. Not for the first time, I consider sneaking out to pop over to Declan's shop to demand answers.

I nearly manage to pluck up the courage when I hear the click of Nonna's heels coming down the stairs. For the first time since the scene with Declan happened at the police station, we're alone and I'm determined to find out what the hell is going on.

She peers around the corner and her eyes widen when they land on me leaning against the counter. "Oh," she says, "I thought you left with your brother."

"Nope. I thought we could talk."

Nonna smoothes a hand over her hair and

frowns. "I don't have time to talk right now, Sullivan. I'm supposed to be in a meeting in twenty minutes."

"You told me that you wanted us to be a family, right? That you wanted for me to trust you? How do you expect me to do that when you won't tell me why you have a problem with Declan? The police interviewed him for Christ's sake. They didn't see any cause for concern, so I don't see why you're so adamant about me staying away from him."

She crosses the kitchen to the coffee machine, taking her time selecting a mug and a little cup of her favorite French roast. She puts the cup in the machine and turns it on. The smell fills the kitchen as I wait for her to respond.

"Did your mother ever tell you what happened to your Poppa Joe?" she asks.

I lean my elbows on the counter. "She said he had a hunting accident when we were very little."

"Well, Declan was with him," Nonna says matter-of-factly.

My mouth opens and closes a couple of times before I manage to say, "He was?"

She nods. "They went on a hunting trip just before Christmas that year. There was a bad snowstorm and they got blocked in the forest. Your Poppa Joe and a couple others, including Declan's father became trapped and Declan had to go for help. He didn't make it in time. Declan and his father's friend Red were the only two to survive the ordeal. The others, along with your grandfather, died from the cold."

A gamut of emotions race through me as I digest the information. No wonder they were so shocked when they saw each other at the police station. Growing up here after dealing with all of that must be why he seems so lonely. Ostracized with no family. I can't imagine how he must have felt. "I didn't know," I tell her.

"I don't hold it against him. He was only a boy at the time. But we still steer clear of each other whenever we run into one another in town. It's just too painful a reminder. I hope you understand."

"I do. Thank you for finally telling me."

"Despite what you may think, Sullivan. The last thing I want is to come between you and someone who makes you happy. I know how fleeting love is, believe me." She rubs my arm and I try not to show how confused I am. I don't want her to think I blame her for what happened with Declan.

"It was only one date." One helluva date. "I was more caught off guard than anything," I say.

"I know you were. I should have told you sooner,

but it's hard for me to talk about, as you can imagine."

"No, I completely understand."

"Thank you, sweetheart." She pulls me into a hug. "Now, I hope this doesn't keep you from seeing him again. Our past aside, I'm sure he's a great man. You were practically floating when you came back from your night with him."

"I don't know, he seemed pretty sure when he said we shouldn't be together."

"Sometimes women have to tell a man what's best for him, sweetheart. They're misguided in that way."

"I'll keep that in mind if I see him again."

She pauses for a second before saying, "I've been meaning to talk to you for a while about a...matter and I haven't quite had the words, but I think now is probably a good time. So we can get everything on the table."

My eyes round and I cross my arms over my chest. "I'm not sure what you mean," I say.

"Of course you do, dear. I'm talking about your gift." I look away as she continues. "I'm assuming you received it after your mother died."

I nod, but I don't say anything. "I'm so sorry that there wasn't anyone there to help guide you through that. I'm certain she wouldn't have wanted that for you."

"So she knew?" I can't help but ask.

"Of course she did. She received hers around her eighteenth birthday, too."

"Could she...did she have the same abilities I do?"

Nonna sits on one of the bar stools and leans her elbows on the kitchen counter. "Everyone's gifts are a little different, just like each person is different. She was especially talented at mind reading, which is part of the reason why she left. She couldn't handle how sad I was after your grandfather died. I couldn't let it go and I wasted away with grief."

So that explains the memory I had of her when I first got here. My heart aches for them both because they never got to mend that rift. I don't want the same to be said for us, so I take the seat next to her at the bar.

"I always thought she could tell when I was lying," I confide.

Nonna laughs fondly. "It's not a fair gift, that's for sure, though I imagine it came in handy raising you and your brother. So tell me, what is yours?"

I can't believe we're having this conversation, but I feel lighter with each word. Knowing that there's someone out there like me, that I still have that connection with my mother, is priceless. "I'm not sure what you would call it, exactly, but when I touch something, it can be a person or something simple like a set of keys, I can sense their memories." I hesitate before saying, "Like when I got here, I saw you and mom arguing when she left."

She nods. "I regret that day very much."

I lay a hand on her arm. "I know you do. And I know that if she were here she'd be glad that we are here with you."

"I'm glad you're here, too." She pats my hand. "This is the only thing I'm going to say on the matter, but I hope you take it to heart. Don't make my mistake. Don't let so much time pass that you aren't able to go back. If Declan is the person you want to be with, then you shouldn't give up, no matter what."

I wish things were that easy. No matter how many times I call or go by, he doesn't want to talk to me and I start to wonder if there isn't something else that he isn't telling me.

Chapter Eight
Sully

It happened on the way to my internship at the Chronicle a couple weeks later. It caught me so off guard I could have been shot and it wouldn't have caused as much of a shock.

I was focused on blowing the steam from my cappuccino, so I didn't see him until it was too late to hide. I look up and find his brown eyes from a few doors down and a shock reverberates through my body. He pauses where he's unlocking the door to his shop, one hand frozen on the knob. My own fingers clutch the uncomfortably hot coffee cup and my feet are rooted to the cracked sidewalk.

His hand falls from the doorknob and he takes a hesitant step towards me. A bud of hope blooms in my chest and steals the breath from my lungs. In spite of everything Sam and Nonna have said over the past few weeks and in spite of my own pep talks, a voice in my head has a short prayer on repeat. My mouth opens and closes.

I finally make up my mind to cross the few shop fronts between us and make amends, *do something,* when he seems to come to his senses. His hand goes back to the knob, twists, and he sends one last long look over his shoulder before he disappears into the dark recesses of his store.

I take a step backward like I've been dealt a physical blow and damn if it doesn't feel like it. This is why girls like me stay in our safe little bubbles with our predictable lives. Mysterious, handsome strangers aren't worth the risk, no matter how good they can kiss.

Giving myself a shake, I step into the office and greet Michelle at the desk. Staff is minimal today due to the incoming storms. The normally bright and boisterous newsroom is eerily quiet. So quiet that I can hear the hum from the fax machine and the tapping of the few people who are at their desks. The whole room is darkened by the bruised clouds rolling in.

As I make my way toward my desk I'm grateful I

only have to do a couple hours' worth of busy work before I can leave. I'd hate to get caught out in a thunderstorm.

Leroy spots me immediately and beelines for my desk. His tie is especially atrocious today, a puke and burnt orange creation which looks like it came straight out of the eighties.

"Great!" he says, running his fingers over his mustache. "We've just received the coroner's report for the Swift River girl's murder. Apparently it was some kind of animal mauling. Give me a report on recent animal attacks in the area, then go down and take some pictures of the crime scene for me before the weather gets too bad."

I glance out the window at the increasingly black sky and mask my frown. "Right away, sir."

Hannah, another one of the lucky students from Hastings offers to help, but I brush her off. Searching the Chronicle's database for previous attacks shouldn't take me long.

My workspace isn't much more than a miniature desk crammed into a corner, but I'd managed to brighten it up with cute little baskets and bright colors. A picture of my parents sits right next to my laptop.

As I search the database, I take a quick sip of

coffee, burning my tongue. The search returns over thirty results, the majority of which seem to be regarding small animal attacks. Snakes, insects and spiders. A shiver skates down my spine at the thought of traipsing through the forest with them later, but I brush that off.

A dozen or so of the results are from larger animals. A couple of bears, some cougars and then there are a few news reports that make me pause, put down my coffee, and sit up a little straighter in my chair. The unidentified attacks left the victims nearly eviscerated by claw and bite marks from an unnamed animal. I flash back to the blood-soaked dirt and horribly mangled body and the coffee sours in my stomach.

After a few moments, I manage to calm my queasy stomach and put together a list of the reports and references for Leroy. I hope he has second thoughts about sending me out there when he reads them. Wanting to be thorough—and to satiate a bit of my curiosity—I expand the search to the neighboring county. It turns up more of the small animal attacks, and I'm shocked to find nearly double that of the large, unidentified animal attack claims.

How many things are in that forest, exactly? Or maybe I should be asking *what* is in that forest?

Rain follows me across town, and by the time I make it to Swift River, it's coming down with a vengeance. Thunder crashes and electricity zips across my skin. The scent of metal carries on the rushing wind and goosebumps rise on my exposed flesh.

I may be overreacting, but after recounting the list of vicious things ready to attack me at any moment, I don't want to go into the forest unarmed. Plus, Sam's warnings are playing in the back of my head about a madman being loose. After a quick search through the truck, I come up with the tire iron. Not much it will do against a mountain lion or some shit, but at least it is something.

I carry it in my right hand, my left grips an increasingly unsteady umbrella. The canopy of trees protects me for the most part and I can only hope that the scene hasn't been completely washed away yet. Leroy has it out for me as it is, the last thing he needs is a reason to get rid of me.

I see another cluster of rocks and I catch myself before I can smile. Unbidden, the memory of the first time I met Declan plays across my mind. *"I'm sorry to put you through this, Sullivan. It won't happen again."* He is right about that. Maybe it would have been better if we'd never met.

By the time I make it to the area marked off by police tape, I'm over the wind and rain and edgy feeling I always get now when I'm in the forest alone. I hope Leroy sees the rain and gloom as contributing to the atmosphere instead of a shoddy job on my part.

A few minutes later, I'm powering down the camera when I hear the tornado sirens sound in the distance.

I whirl and lose grip on the tire iron, it bounces off a tree and ricochets in the distance, obscured by the rain and encroaching darkness. *Fuck.* Despite the rain drenching my best gray slacks and certainly rendering my white shirt see-through, my mouth runs dry at the thought of not making it to shelter before the tornado hits. God, what the hell was I thinking?

I remember Declan's cabin is somewhere around here and turn in the direction I hope it's in and run.

The low heels I'm wearing don't serve my purpose well and within a few seconds I've managed to twist my ankle. I don't know how long I manage to limp through the forest. Long enough that my shoes become a distant memory. Long enough that my feet are cracked and bloodied. For the first time since I started my mad dash through the woods, I feel the tendrils of fear snake through my chest.

The sweet refuge of the Indiana woodland I'd enjoyed with Declan no longer seemed tranquil and relaxing. The sound of the rustling leaves and the distant crack of lightning in the distance are no longer the marks of a warm summer night. Instead they are the crunch of destruction heading my way. Fingers of felled tree branches scrape at the skin of my bare arms and grasp at my button up shirt. My toes catch in the soft clay of the forest floor. The tender soles of my feet power through endless pine needles and cones, but I'm too overwhelmed to care.

Every movement in the darkness around me causes my heart to stutter in my chest. Even the soft whisper of wind carries the threat of death.

Rivulets of rain cause my clothes to slick to my skin. Adrenaline too alternates between flashes of intense heat and nausea and stomach-dropping hollowness. I begin to grow incredibly drowsy and short of breath. My chest aches with the need for oxygen and my arms grow heavy. My injured feet drag on the ground and I lose my footing on more than one occasion.

Chilled air whips around me with renewed

vengeance. It roves through the darkness rustling branches and swirling leaves, a harrowing and empty symphony of dread.

A scream ripped straight from my nightmares echoes through the corpses of trees and brings me to a screeching halt. The same one that I heard in the memory the day I discovered that poor girl's body.

I whip around in all directions thinking maybe there's someone like me trapped in the woods. It sounded like a woman's voice.

I strain my ears over the sound of the howling wind for another sign. My heartbeat thuds too loudly and my lungs heave for breath. I can't hear anything. A few seconds pass and I chalk the sound up to an animal in distress, so I press on, my exhaustion having caught up with me in the few moments of pause.

A few yards more and I manage to find a trail. I'm not certain where it leads, but anywhere would be an immeasurable blessing at this point. If I'm lucky, it'll be the trail leading to the tourist center. If I'm not, well...I brush that thought from my mind.

I hear a loud *snap* of a branch near me and I whirl around, blood rushing to my head. My eyes strain into the distance, trying to detect abnormal movements in the shadows. The only thing I can see are trees and more trees, all of them bending wildly in the wind.

I take a few steps, my feet now completely numb, when I hear the scream again. This time from right behind me. I turn to investigate and see a shadow weaving through the trees.

The hairs on my nape rise and tingle. This isn't a person in trouble, my gut tells me. This isn't someone who needs my help. Rather than stay to find out, I run like hell in the other direction.

As I run, the screams start up again, only this time I can hear them coming from every direction simultaneously. Over the sound of my heart and breaths and feet slamming on the ground, I can hear the telltale sounds of someone—or something—in pursuit. I remember the reports of hikers being mauled and I pray that I won't become one of them. The face of the girl laying in the weeds haunts me.

I want to cry, I want to scream, I want to be somewhere, *anywhere* else. Screams echo in my head, obliterating the sound of everything else. Whatever is out there is taunting me, enjoying the thrill of my fear.

My weak ankle catches on a branch and I face-plant into a puddle of brackish water. The voices come to a stop and I scramble on my knees to hide behind the fat trunk of a tree. Maybe I'm going fucking crazy. Maybe losing my parents was too much.

As the crunching sound of feet approaches, I almost hope it's the tornado coming to take me out of this hell-hole.

Chapter Nine
Declan

I'd been avoiding her because I knew exactly how I would react if I was alone with her again. Hell, we were separated by what essentially amounts to an entire building and I can still smell the perfume on her skin. I can hear her heart skip a beat when she notices I am staring at her and damn the responding thud of my own.

I nearly stride across the sidewalk to her, to make up for being a jackass, when I remember exactly why I pushed her away in the first place. A flash of pain crosses her face when she sees me hesitate and I push my way inside the store before I give in to that look. She should stay far, far away from a dangerous man like me. She's too sweet and innocent.

I would ruin her. Even worse, I *want* to ruin her.

Red frowns at me when I enter and I hold up a hand on my way back to the office. "Don't start."

"Don't tell me what to do, boy. I'll damn well start whatever I like."

"Well, don't let it bother you if I don't listen while you do."

"Suzanna Thomas' granddaughter? What the hell were you thinking?"

"I wasn't thinking anything."

"You mean your dick was doing all the decision making."

"Fuck off. I've got work to do."

He makes a sound in his throat. "Won't be anything left to do when that woman wipes your skinny little ass out of Hillsborough."

"Don't worry, I handled it."

"I'm just looking out for you, son."

I duck my head into my hands. "I know you are. I don't mean to be such a dick. Just been a long morning."

Thunder rattles and our heads both swivel to the windows. "Gonna be a bitch of a storm. All the tours canceled for today. You're gonna want to get closed up soon before it gets too bad. Not going to get any of that work done today. You'll have to find something else to keep you busy."

"You get on home, Red. I'll handle things here."

Red nods and heads out before stopping at my office door. "And by something else to keep you busy, I don't mean going to find that girl."

I curl my lips at him, but don't respond. The little amount of paperwork I have to do can wait. Urgency lights my blood, probably caused by the coming storm, and I decide to go ahead and pack up. As I'm leaving, I note the Chronicle employees are filing out, too. I pause by the shop door under the guise of locking up as I look over to try and catch another glimpse of Sullivan.

When the last person leaves and takes out a set of keys to lock the door tension tightens the muscles in my gut. Has she already left?

Recognizing the girl as another one of the Hastings kids, probably in Sully's class, I jog over and offer a friendly, "Hey! Some weather, huh?"

She looks up and smiles. "Looks like it's going to head this way, yeah."

I try to act casual and fail miserably. "Sully make it out okay?"

"I think so. Leroy had her run over to the last crime scene a few minutes ago, but she should have made it home. I don't think she'd risk it in this weather."

She was probably right. Then again, Sully didn't seem like the type of person to give up that easily.

Both the girl and I look at each other in alarm when the sirens start going off. She doesn't have time to react before I'm racing back to my truck.

Thank fuck the crime scene is near my cabin. I break about twenty laws as I speed across town. The sky is angry and dark and my skin is prickling with the need to shift. My teeth lengthen and my mouth waters, but I manage to keep the change back by sheer will. I need to get to the park first. Then I can let go.

I'll never be able to forgive myself if something happens to her because of all this shit. A growl rips through my throat and vibrates throughout the cab of the truck.

I make it to the park in record time and explode from the truck, ripping off my shirt as I go. The only other times I managed to shift were in times of high stress or emotion. Normally, I can't control the change, but as I dive into the forest on all fours I manage to keep my senses about me through the change. It surprises me enough that I skid to a stop for a moment and look down at my fur covered body.

A scream rips through the air and I plunge into the trees after the sound, sniffing the air for a trace of her scent. I find signs of her walk on the trail and my heart stills when I hear the sounds of the tornado pulling up trees and brush behind me.

I see the yellow tape in the distance and push myself to go faster. Her scent gets stronger the closer I get. I leap over the taped off area and land on the other side. A few feet away, I spot her white shirt huddled in a ditch.

Even though I know revealing myself to her will put both of us in danger, I would rather her know my secret than risk losing her.

Without giving myself time to think, I race toward her curled body and scoop her into my arms before she has a chance to see me coming. She surprises me by not reacting other than to curl herself closer to my warmth. She's shaking from fear, her eyes wild and confused, but she turns to me on instinct. The beast in me fucking loves that, and I know he'll never let her go now that she's come to him for protection.

I've been through these woods enough during my tours and in my shifted form that I know every inch. There's an empty tourist building not far from here. I know it's strong enough to withstand the weather so I head in its direction. Her fingers are curled into my fur and her heart races against my chest. I just hope I can get us both there in one piece.

When the trees part and I spot the building in the distance I double my speed. The wind pulls, and I don't need to turn around to know that the vortex is just behind me. In the moments before I reach the building, time seems to stop. I give one last push of speed and propel us through a large plate glass window.

Sharp pain bites through my shoulder, but I roll off of my side and get to my feet. The storm cellar beneath us is the safest place and we have seconds before that won't even matter anymore.

Using my shoulder, I push through the cellar door, slamming it behind us just as the storm reaches the building. The cellar is pitch black and Sully shivers against me. I have the presence of mind to set her down on a chair I'm able to find in the dark. Once she's settled, I take several steps back, putting as much distance between us as I can.

The intensity of the moment allowed me to focus on getting Sullivan safe. Now that I'm locked in a room as a tornado ravages the forest around us, I'm more worried about keeping her safe...from me.

My guttural breaths are the only sound in the small enclosed space. I drop down to my haunches in an effort to focus my racing thoughts and control the urge to completely give in to the beast inside of me. Through sheer will I manage to pull back from the edge. My claws and teeth retract. Skin replaces fur and I crumple to my knees from the strain and rush of adrenaline. *She's safe.*

I nearly jump out of my skin when I feel the soft, hesitant touch of her fingers on my shoulder. My whole body shivers and tenses. I press the flats of my claw-like hands into the cement to keep from reacting. I don't know if I want to shove her away or put them around her to hold her close again. My beast liked having her little body against me entirely too much. Even now, he's growling to be let out completely, to make her his.

"Don't touch me," I whisper harshly. Her hand contracts on my shoulder before she releases and takes a few steps backwards.

"Declan?" she asks. "That's you, isn't it? Oh my god. How did...what did...what *are* you?"

"Not now." I grit my teeth together. "Stay over there."

I can sense her fear even though she moves to the other side of the small room. "Are we going to be safe here? I heard the tornado sirens."

"You'll be safe from the storm," I say.

"And from you?"

"I guess we'll find out."

I hear her swallow. "You're not going to hurt me," she says, even though her voice quavers.

"As long as you stay over there you should be fine." I don't know how true that statement is. She was probably doomed the moment I set eyes on her.

"What about you? Are you okay?"

"Don't worry about me."

"I'm sick of people deciding what's best for me. I'll worry about you if I damn well please. I can feel the blood on my shirt and I know it's not from me. Now tell me if you're okay."

"None of it will matter if this place doesn't hold up through the storm. Be quiet so I can hear if it's passed."

I hear her growl a little in her throat and the muscles in my stomach clench. Even though we're in danger and I know I should be putting as much distance between us as I can, I still want her. If my beast had his way, we would have already been tumbling on the ground.

I concentrate on my surroundings. I can hear the hum of the generator that must have kicked on after the power went down. The fact that it's still here and intact is a good sign. Through the wall of concrete, I can hear the howl of the wind. Rolls of thunder vibrate the structure above us and I hear the crack of branches succumbing to the storm.

When I refocus back on the room the first thing I notice is that Sullivan is standing right next to me. I jerk backward against the wall, but there's nowhere to go.

"I need you to do something for me," I say firmly.

She takes a few steps toward me, but I back away. "Anything," she tells me.

"Walk away. Right now." But she doesn't. She continues getting closer "Sully, go."

"I can't," she whispers.

"Why not?"

"There's nowhere else I'd rather be," she says, just as I hear the tornado reach the building.

Chapter Ten
Sully

One second I'm cowering behind a tree, certain that I'm about to be sucked into oblivion and the next a shadow comes rushing at me, scooping me up into its arms. Exhaustion and fear have run riot on my emotions and I can barely keep my eyes open as it races through the forest. The only thing I know is that it smells safe, it smells like Declan.

I wrap my arms around it and my hands come in contact with his neck. The thoughts and feelings come at me like a shot to the gut. I can see and hear everything around us. I can sense the tornado not far behind and all of the animals fleeing in front. But the thing that strikes me the most is the same thought that keeps repeating in his brain.

Keep her safe.

We make it to some sort of building that I don't recognize and down to a cellar that I hope will withstand the tornado. He sets me down and backs away. I crumple against the wall, my whole body feeling like I've been hit by a truck.

I rub a hand at my eyes and when I look up the thing that saved me is Declan, shirtless, by the door. Which completely blows my mind, even when I consider the crazy shit that I've been through the past few weeks. I barely have time to sort through that information before he's on top of me as the tornado finally hits.

I cover my ears as the wind whistles through the air. The ceiling above us shakes with the force of multiple impacts and Declan's warm body presses me even closer to the cold concrete beneath me. Rumbles come with each of his exhalations and I focus on that instead of the disaster happening one floor up.

What feels like an eternity later, the wind finally dies down and the silence is deafening. Declan slowly moves from on top of me and scoots with lightning quickness across the room. I can see the way his body shakes even through the darkness. I fight my own growing panic and confusion. Nonna's words replay in my head. I don't know if what we had will last, but it sure as hell deserves the chance to try.

"Are you okay?"

"I'm going to be honest here for your own well-being." He fights a full-body shiver. "I can't control myself much longer. So you need to go before I can't control it anymore."

"Was this why you pushed me away that day?" I take a step forward, but stop when a growl reverberates throughout the dark room. "What...I mean I can't believe I'm saying this, but what are you? How did we get here so fast? How did you know where I was?"

"Sully, please. Don't come any closer. I don't want to hurt you."

"You could have hurt me when we were alone that night and you didn't." I take another step and ignore the flash of his now razor-sharp teeth.

"I was relaxed that night." He groans. "You don't understand."

"Then, please, make me understand. You owe me that since you gave me a shit explanation about not wanting to see me again."

"Don't you get it? You could end up like that girl in the woods and I won't risk that. You're too..."

I take another step. His body is nearly vibrating with the urge to keep still. "I'm too what?" I whisper.

He drops his head against the wall with a groan. "You're too important to me."

"If you're so out-of-control, then how did you manage to find me and bring me to safety? How did you manage to keep control of yourself during the tornado? You're not making any sense."

"Please leave," comes his ravaged whisper.

The last step brings me within reaching distance and I finally get a good look at him. I control my reaction so that I don't spook him even more than he already is. His face is sharper, more defined and his hair has thickened to cover most of his jawline and his eyes are no longer the soft amber that I remembered. Now they're a bright gold that damn near glows in the darkness, like they did that night in the clearing when he kissed me. His thickly muscled arms that are now covered in light fur. His thighs have ripped through his pants and he lost his shoes somewhere in the forest. My brain trips over the scene in front of me, but after my own surprise magical discovery, I manage to keep my calm.

"You—you're some sort of shapeshifter?" In front of my own eyes his face morphs into something both man and beast. He lets out a groan. The concrete under his hands has deep slashes from where he's clawed through in an effort to keep still. "This is why you pushed me away?"

"I should have never kissed you," he says, his chest heaving. "I should have walked away that day."

"I don't think you're going to hurt me."

"You shouldn't be so sure of that."

"But I am."

He shakes his head, seeming to disagree with my words. "We've spent one night together, Sully. You can't possibly know that."

"I know you came to save me. I know that instead of putting me at risk, you walked away to save me and spared hurting my grandmother. Those are the actions of someone I can trust." I kneel before him and reach out a hand to touch his shoulder. "I trust you not to hurt me, Declan."

He shudders at the contact, his neck arching up. When he looks back down at me his eyes are molten. He seems to struggle with himself before reaching out to me and pulling me into his lap, my legs thrown over one thigh and his arm cradles my back.

I cup his face with one hand. "This isn't too bad, is it?" Then I gasp as I realize I can sense him in this form. I see myself crouched by the tree from his point of view. I hear him thinking *Keep her safe* and I remember the gentle way he held me in his arms.

"You have no idea," he growls. "I can smell you like this. It's driving me crazy touching you right now."

"Do you want me to move?" I start to get out of his lap, but his grip tightens around me.

"No!" he barks out. "I don't know if it's safe out there yet. Let's give it a few minutes."

"Okay, we'll wait." I rest my head on his chest and take a calming breath. "There's something I should probably tell you, too. Something about me."

"If it's about your grandfather, I—"

I put a hand on his cheek and look into his eyes. "No, my grandmother explained. It's not that, it's something else."

"What is it?" His hand runs up and down my back, soothing me, even though I bet he doesn't realize it.

"My family...apparently we all have these...gifts." I don't look at him as I speak. "After my parents died in the car accident, I started to be able to sense... things. If I touch something, I can get these visions of things that happened around it in the past or if someone touched it recently, I know their thoughts and things like that. And..."

"Go on," he says.

"Well it's one of the things that drew me to you in the first place," I confess. "I haven't been handling it very well and the night of the party, I was overwhelmed by everything. If I touch someone, you see, I can understand what they're thinking or sometimes I get memories from their past." I swallow thickly before continuing and the hand at my back doesn't stop its gentle strokes. "The first time you touched me, I didn't want the gift anymore. I hated it. Then, it didn't work on you. I didn't know what you were thinking. It was like I was free from this curse. It was so nice to be with you without being bombarded by your thoughts."

"So that's why you were interested in me?" he asks, his voice low.

"No! God no. I liked *you*. I like that you seem so big and bad, but you have this other soft side that I think no one else gets to see. I like that your first instinct is always to protect me. I like what we started and I don't want to give that up. My grandmother told me that you should never let people you care about walk away, so this is me. Not letting you walk away."

"I need to touch you now. Just," his breathing

gets rougher, "just tell me if it's too much. I'll stop. I can stop."

I use the hand on his cheek to guide his face down to mine. He buries his lips in my throat, the hair tickling the soft skin there. As soon as his lips touch my throat the world around us melts away. He nuzzles, moving his body over mine until I'm flat on my back with him above me.

His thick forearm cushions my head from the rough ground and I forget the rest. I try to keep my eyes open, try to learn this foreign side of him, but he nips my skin and my eyes grow weary of focusing on the darkness around us. When he pulls away I peer up at him and find that the fur covering his face has receded and his eyes are back to the soft amber hue.

"Hey," I whisper, smiling up at him.

I expect him to say something sweet, like he did the night of our date. Instead he frowns at me and says, "If you ever do anything as crazy as going out during a tornado warning again, I will personally beat your ass."

"I'd like to see you try."

He leans back on his haunches and winces. I remember the blood on my shirt and get to my feet. "We need to get you somewhere we can look at that wound. Your house is nearby. Do you think you can make it?"

"I'm fine. Let's just hope it's still there." Declan helps me to my feet, pausing to press a soft, sweet kiss to my lips that leaves me breathless once again.

"You aren't mad about me not telling you about my gift are you?"

"As long as you're not mad about having to date a man who occasionally likes to run around like a bear, then no."

My heart soars as he leads me up the stairs. The door is blocked by some debris on the other side, but Declan demonstrates another trait that goes along with his ability to shift into a bear: super strength. He braces his feet on the step and heaves with bulging arms. After two or three pushes that leave my jaw on the floor, he manages to dislodge what turns out to be a huge trunk from where it lay on top of the door.

He helps me out of the stairwell and sets me down on the ground. The old building is essentially nonexistent. Remnants of the wood and furniture lay around us in a dump. Like it was a child's block tower that had gotten knocked over. There are no roofs, no walls. Everything has been ripped apart and strewn in every direction across the clearing.

"C'mon," Declan says, lifting me up into his arms.

"Whoa. I would comment on whether or not you could carry me, but I just saw you move a tree the size of a small country."

He grins, but I can tell he's in pain.

"Are you sure it won't bother your arm?" I ask.

"Sully, I'll be fine. I just want to get you home where I know you're safe."

I gesture with an arm. "Lead the way."

He lopes through the clearing with an easy grace that I wouldn't have expected from such a big man. When I look away from his handsome face and see just how fast we're going, I yelp, throwing my hands around his neck. I hear his responding chuckle in my ear.

The next time I look up we're bounding up the steps to his cabin. He sets me down carefully by his door. He holds onto me with one hand as he unlocks the door with the other and leads me inside.

He kisses my shoulder and moves past me to the dining room table where he dumps a bunch of medical supplies.

"Wow, you're pretty well stocked up. Does this happen often?"

He shrugs and winces when it jostles the gash on his shoulder. "Sometimes."

"Sometimes?"

"Well, I don't always remember what happens when I shift. Sometimes I wake up to find myself covered in things like this. I've gotten used to doing quick patch jobs." He sends me a rueful smile.

I cross to his side and take the antibacterial wash from him. "I'll help."

"You don't have to do that," he says.

"You didn't have to save me," I respond. He sits quietly, his shoulders bowed. My mouth opens and closes a few times before I manage to find the right words. "How long have you been able to do that, exactly?" I ask.

He straightens and looks up at me, those big brown eyes hiding all of his thoughts. "Since I was fourteen. The first time I ever shifted was on the night my father died. I was trying to save him."

"What happened?" I deftly clean the wound and apply antibacterial ointment and a bandage.

"It's a long story."

I move around to his front and he tugs me down to his lap. "Was your father a shifter, too?"

"I assume so, but I never really asked my grand-father about it after he died. By the time I was old enough to get it under control, he'd passed and then there was no one left."

"So you had to go through all of that alone?" That couldn't have been easy on an orphaned fourteen-year-old. The thought of it makes me want to go and hug him.

"I did all right," he says, his shoulders bunched up around his ears as I bandage the wound.

"All done," I say. I figure we've both had enough of the serious topics for today.

"Thanks. That should do it."

He disposes of the wrappings in the trash and disappears into the bathroom to replace the supplies. "We should be okay if you need me to take you back home."

I shake my head. "I don't think so. You have a lot of time to make up for, mister. You never gave me a second date. Unless you consider rescuing damsels a date."

He stays across the room. "I'm still not sure if it's a good idea for you to stay here."

"You don't really have a choice unless you want to throw me out. I told you I trust you."

Declan moves closer. "You aren't going to give up on this are you?"

I smile. "Nope."

"I'm pretty wiped," he admits. "Would it be too boring if I suggested we go take a nap? A long one."

"No, that sounds like a great idea."

I follow Declan down the hall to his bedroom. It's not very big, but the views into the forest make up for any lack in square footage. The windows nearly cover one wall and when he tugs me down onto the bed, I realize that it's almost like sleeping outside.

He curls around my back and the warmth emanating from his chest combined with the crash from the adrenaline makes me yawn. His arms wrap around my middle and pull me close. I sigh in contentment.

"You still owe me that fishing trip," he mumbles in my hair. "Don't think I forgot."

I fall asleep with a smile on my face.

Chapter Eleven
Sully

The next morning, I wake up in Declan's bed with his arms wrapped around me.

Declan starts nuzzling the back of my neck. "Good morning," he murmurs.

I can't help my responding smile. "Good morning."

His hand rides low on my hip. I'd lost my mud-slicked pants and shirt in favor of one of his T-shirts. He's so tall that it comes to mid-thigh on me. I feel the heat of his hand burning through the material.

He rolls me to my back and props himself up on one arm. At first I think he's going to say something, then I realize that the air around us has grown incredibly thick with tension. My breath shallows in my chest and I grip the material of the sheet by my side. Slowly, so slowly that it drives me out of my mind, he leans down to press his lips to mine.

My eyes slide closed and I unclench the sheet to slide my fingers into his hair. With my other hand I urge him to move until his weight is completely on top of me. The sensation feels so incredible that I groan into his mouth, my lips parting to accept his tongue in one commanding thrust.

He breaks the kiss to breathe heavily into my neck. "You need to tell me to stop," he says into my throat.

"I don't want you to stop," I whisper-groan.

I can't think about anything aside from the feeling of him nibbling at my earlobe and how goddamn good it feels to have his weight press me into the bed. I spread my legs to bring him closer. The shirt rides up my hips leaving only the thin material of my panties and the cloth of his briefs between us.

"Damn, baby, I can smell you already." Declan traces the line of my throat with his tongue. His mouth charts a path down my collar bone to the rigid point of my nipple underneath his shirt. "You smell like the best sex, and it's even better because you've already got me all over you." He growls, his teeth nipping through the material of his shirt to take my nipple into his mouth.

I throw my head back against the pillow as he dampens the shirt with swirls of his tongue and nips of his teeth. His mouth trails along my chest until he reaches my other breast and pays his undivided attention there as well.

He noses his way down the shirt, the two damp spots tweaking my already sensitive nipples with cool air. I've never moved so fast with a guy before. I've never felt comfortable enough in bed to let a man take control like this. But like I told him the day before, I trust him and it's incredibly freeing.

His teeth nip at the line of my panties and my body flashes white-hot. He licks a path down the center seam, throwing my legs over his broad shoulders and arching me wide. He slides the material of my panties over so that I'm bared to his gaze. His free hand delves into my swollen, slippery folds and I cry out, arching my back against him.

I can't control the movement of my hips as his fingers explore everywhere but the center of my need. My head writhes back and forth as he teases me and my hands drag the material of the shirt up and over. I hiss out a breath as cool air greets my heated flesh.

His head comes up and he whispers his approval, his eyes glowing bright gold again. My hands go to my breasts as he kneels between my legs, his fingers finally stroking deep, though not as fast as I need to quell the rising heat.

When a slick, wet heat flicks across my clit the muscles in my legs turn to water and my hips fall open, my legs thrusting them closer to the source of pleasure. "Declan, I need..."

He presses a kiss to my thigh. "I know what you need."

"Please. I need you inside."

"I know you do, but first I want to watch you come for me again. I want to feel you come under my hands. I want to taste you on my tongue."

He adds another finger, this time picking up the pace and stroking even more deeply. He brings his mouth back, his tongue doing wicked things to wring high-pitched cries from my throat. But I can't seem to get quite where I need to, can't seem to open my legs wide enough or take him as deep as I need him.

Declan pauses his devastating assault to wrench my panties down and off of my legs. He settles back down with one hand lifting my hips to his mouth. He adds a third finger, hooking them in such a way that something sparks inside of me. Then, I can't breathe, can't think, can't even see as his tongue flicks me over the breaking point. I can feel myself growing wetter, the slickness causing a sweet friction that devastates me as much as his tongue and fingers.

He climbs up my body, hooking my legs over his hips as he reaches in his nightstand for a condom. I take it from his hands, ripping it open and sliding it down his long, firm length. My eyes squeeze shut in anticipation of having him inside of me. If he's that talented with his tongue, sex with him is probably going to kill me.

He fits himself between my legs again and leans down to kiss me. The taste of us mingles and I can feel myself clenching, needy, in anticipation. When he breaks the kiss, I arch against him, swiveling my hips in invitation. One of his hands holds me steady, the other grips his thick length as he brings himself to my entrance. He pushes in with one, firm glide and my mouth drops open in shock, a soundless cry of undeniable pleasure. Already sensitive from his earlier attention it doesn't take much for him to stoke the fire back to life.

His forehead drops to the pillow beside me and he whispers, "God, you feel amazing. Perfect."

Unable to put into words what I'm feeling, I bring his lips back to mine for another kiss. I groan into his mouth as my muscles start fluttering around him. He deepens his thrusts, grinding against me, pinning my legs under his arms to hit just the right spot to take me there again. I whimper into his mouth with each thrust as my body tenses.

When I come to, he's smiling above me as he moves slowly, letting me recover from the second best orgasm *of my life.*

"Don't worry," he says, "I've been waiting a long time to find a woman like you, Sullivan Thomas. I've got you all to myself today and I'm going to make it last."

"I knew you were the one for me the day I saw you in the forest," Declan says a couple hours later after we've both recovered, then started all over again, then recovered for the last time. "I wouldn't have taken you to Antonio's if you weren't important to me."

"What do you mean?"

He kisses my knuckles, then holds them to his chest above the beat of his heart. "That was where they went on their first date."

Confusion, exhaustion and adrenaline have made my thought processes slow to a sluggish pace. I shake my head to try and clear it. "Who went on their first date?"

"My parents."

I press a hand to my nervous stomach. "It was?"

Declan rolls us so that I'm back in the crook of his arm. "The restaurant was new back then, it had just opened. Dad wanted to impress her so he paid Antonio a shit load of money to serenade Mom, even though Antonio had never done that before. Ever since I was a kid I've wanted to take a woman there. I knew I would, but I never met the right one." He stops and turns back to me, his eyes are now an amber color that I can see even in the dim light. "Until you."

"Sully," he says and I suck in a breath at how much I like it when he says that name, "when I met you, before I knew who you were, the only thing I could think was that I wanted to know what made you look so sad. I've never felt that way about a woman before. When I found out who you were it damn near killed me to walk away from you."

"Me, too," I whisper. Tension coils inside me.

"I don't know if you can forgive me for what happened."

I shake my head, interrupting him. "It wasn't your fault, Declan. You were just a boy."

"I was fourteen, Sully. Old enough to know better. I should have been able to do something."

I roll over onto his chest so that I can look him in the eyes. "There was nothing you could do. I know my grandfather would never hold you responsible. You need to forgive yourself. I know I already have."

"But your family..." The scent of fresh soap wafts around me and I have to resist the urge to bury my nose in his shoulder to drink it up.

"It was my grandmother's idea for me to fight for you. She forgives you, too. You're the one that needs to accept it and forgive yourself," I whisper.

"I don't know if I can."

I place my hand over his heart. "After my parents died, I was lost for a long time. It wasn't until I met you that I remembered what it was like to truly live again. I know you, I've been inside your head, remember? You're a good man, a good son. Your family would want you to be happy."

He takes my lips in another kiss and I let myself get lost in it. For now, that will have to be enough.

Chapter Twelve
Declan

Having Sully in my bed, her scent on my sheets, her sweet body wrapped around me is better than any of my dreams. Hell, it beats all of my fantasies, too. I don't deserve someone this sweet, this innocent, but now that I have her, I'm not letting her go. When a knock comes at the door a few hours later all I want to do is throw the covers over our heads and stay wrapped up in her forever.

Then the knocks turn into someone pounding on the door and they shout, "I know she's here, Cain. Open up."

Sully sits straight up in bed holding the sheet at her breasts. Her tawny hair is mussed, her lips are swollen and there's a bit of beard burn on the underside of her jaw. I've never seen anyone look more beautiful.

"Oh my God, is that my brother?" she screeches, struggling with the sheets to get out of bed.

I thwart her efforts by tugging her back on top of me. She squawks out a noise that makes me smile. Once I have her attention, I say, "Relax. You get dressed while I answer the door. Your clothes should be dry by now."

Her head swivels around. "Where in the hell are my panties?"

I chuckle, feeling strangely at ease, and hold her still long enough for another drugging kiss. "I tossed them somewhere in that direction." I point towards the dresser as I roll out of bed. I pull on a pair of jeans and a T-shirt. I had a feeling Sullivan's brother wouldn't like seeing me au natural.

He pounds on the door again just as I open it. He looks me over, dropping his raised arm. "Sullivan here?" he asks.

I jerk my head inside and say, "She'll be right out. You want some coffee?"

"No, I don't want any coffee. I want to make sure my sister is okay."

I'm surprised by how much he looks like Sullivan, even though she'd mentioned that they were twins. They have the same eyes, same nose, and the same flinty look that says they won't take any shit. I let him size me up as I get a cup ready for him anyway, knowing that I would do the same if I had a sister. Hell even more so, considering the way our first date went.

Sullivan comes out as I'm handing him his cup. "Ohh, coffee," she says, stealing it from me for a sip and burning her tongue in the process. "Shit, that's disgusting. I don't know how you drink it black."

"You scared me. You just disappeared. I thought something had happened to you," Sam says, pulling her into a hug.

"I'm fine, I'm sorry. I should have called."

He breathes out a sigh and gives her one last squeeze. "I'm just glad you're okay."

He lets her go and she comes to my side, taking my mug. I steal a kiss as payment for the coffee and slouch onto one of the chairs in my dining room.

Sam watches with careful eyes as Sully sits next to me, mug in hand. "Look, you seem like a nice guy," he starts, "so I wanted to be the first person to tell you."

Sully's shoulders stiffen. "Tell us what?"

Her brother leans against the kitchen counter and sighs. "They found another body while they were cleaning up the tornado. It was in the woods, near where the found the last one." Sam angles a meaningful look at me.

"That's impossible," Sully says. "We were there yesterday, Sam. There wasn't—"

When Sully breaks off and glances at me sharply, I say, "What's wrong?"

"I—well I thought I was going crazy. I just, it couldn't have been...I mean I was terrified, for fuck's sake there was a tornado behind me."

I take her hand in mine. I can feel my chest going tight with the urge to turn, to protect what's mine, but I breathe deeply until it passes. "You're okay. You're not going crazy. Just take a deep breath and tell me what happened."

Her lips quiver and I notice she's lost the pink glow a morning of sex had given her. "Before you showed up, um, in the woods, I thought I heard someone screaming. I thought I heard someone— something—following me."

My insides turn to a block of ice. "Are you sure you didn't just hear me?"

"No, I'm sure. This happened before you got there. And this was different. It almost sounded like it was circling around me. Like an animal." She pauses, glances at both of us before continuing, "It felt like it was hunting me. I brushed it off at the time, because, well I thought I was just hearing things with the weather and all. I just thought I was scared out of my mind. I didn't know—"

Could the thing targeting people in Hillsborough be another shifter? I know there are others in town, I've seen some of them on my strolls in the woods, but I've never gotten chummy with any of them, considering my past. Most of them like to keep their distance. If a rogue shifter is stalking the woods, it's a goddamn miracle I didn't find her dead body like the others.

My muscles quiver, the urge to shift renewed. I placate that desire by lifting Sully to my lap and draping her arms over my shoulders. Just having her hands on me calms me down. "Of course you didn't, baby. This wasn't your fault, either."

"Something is going on out there, right?" Sam says. "It has to be some kind of animal. A bear maybe?"

Sully and I share a look and I send her a wink. "It could be, maybe." Though I know based on the markings that it wasn't. It has to be something else. Even though I knew it wasn't me attacking those girls, seeing their autopsy reports during the interrogation did help alleviate some of the guilt I felt.

"Either way, I'm going to have to go talk to Red, cancel all the trail tours until the cops can get something figured out. In the meantime, why don't you and Sam stay here?"

"I'd like to go with you, if that's okay. Maybe pick up some of my stuff and let Nonna know that I'm okay. Would that be okay with you, Sam?"

"Yeah, sure. I'll just sit on the big guy's couch in case this thing gets a taste for good-looking freshman, like some horror movie serial killer stereotype."

Nearly all the streets are empty as we drive through Hillsborough on the way to my shop. The tornado had stayed on the side of the forest, thank God, so the majority of the city had been spared its destruction. When I get to the shop the windows are dark and the sign on the door says closed.

Sully and I jump out after I park the truck on the street in front. I unlock the door and call, "Hey, Red. You in the back?"

"Yeah, son, in the office."

Relief spears through me. Red likes to roam through the forest at all hours. A part of me thought he may have gotten caught unawares and not made it back.

"Good to see you, you old sonuvabitch. Thought that tornado might have eaten you up and spit you back out."

Red grins. "That silly old side-winder? Not a match for me, boy." He peers around me at Sully standing by my side. "Is this the girl you've been chasing after? My, isn't she sweet?"

They shake hands and Sully freezes, her eyes wide and I curse under my breath. I forgot about her gift. She excuses herself to peek around while I talk shop with Red. "Have you heard?" I ask him.

"About the other one?" When I nod, he frowns, his salt and pepper mustache twitching. "Yeah, the police were by earlier to let us know we should probably close up until they know more about whatever's getting those girls. He's a sneaky bastard, that's for sure. They didn't have any leads and couldn't even decide if it was a human or an animal that was attacking them."

"This is so fucked."

"You got that right." I hesitate before asking what I really came here wanting to know. Red was the only other one to make it out alive that day. When both of my parents died, he was there for me. He'll have answers to calm my fear. Plus, he's the only one close to me that knows about my ability to shift. "Sully and I were talking and think that it might be another shifter attacking these people. Have you heard anything?"

Red's eyes shutter closed, like the do any time that I've brought up my connection to that night. "I haven't heard anything, but I'll keep an eye out." He wipes the sour look off his face and slaps a hand on my back. "You take that girl back home and I'll finish closing up here, okay?"

"Thanks again. Give me a call if you hear of anything."

"Oh, I will do that, Dec," he says cheerfully. He smiles at Sully as we leave, but I can feel his heated, accusing stare on my back.

Chapter Thirteen
Sully

By the time we make it back to Declan's cabin, we're both sick with worry. Just a few weeks ago, we had our life-changing date in the forest. It was a safe place, his haven. Even looking at it feels like a threat, now that I know what lurks in its shadows.

Nonna was fine, thank God. And she even managed a few sentences with Declan. There may be a beast or man stalking Hillsborough, but at least I have a future with him, a future with my family, to look forward to.

I know as soon as we pull up to Declan's drive that something is wrong. His front door is wide-ass open and the car that Nonna gave Sam to use is still in the drive.

Declan puts the truck in park and I dive out of the door, my feet pumping through the gravel to his front door. He reaches me before I'm able to go in to make sure it's just my overactive imagination and that the rock in my gut is for nothing.

Instead, he pushes me behind him and knocks the door the rest of the way open. It slams against the wall to reveal his empty living room. Or what's left of it.

I gasp, taking in the destruction. Glass from lamps and dishes litters the floor. His rug is scrunched to one side and his TV flickers with snow. A hole mars the wall in the dining room. Streaks of blood arc away from the depression and drops of it dot the hardwood floor underneath.

I don't feel my knees buckle, I just find myself hitting the floor hard enough to knock my teeth together. *I can't lose him*, is all I can think. I lost my parents, I lost my future. I can't lose my brother, my twin, too.

Declan investigates his room and the bathroom, but I can feel it in my gut that Sam isn't here. I take a few deep, calming breaths and try to pull myself together. When I'm reasonably sure that I won't faint, I get back to my feet and head to the dining room. The sight of what must be Sam's blood makes me sick, but I choke it down. I don't have time to be sick now.

The drops of blood paint the floor from the hole in the wall to the front door. I follow them down the steps and across the gravel until it disappears in the grassy trail which leads to the forest.

I feel Declan's presence behind me. "He's in the forest," I tell him without turning around. "I have to go after him."

"The hell you are," Declan says, then grabs me by the arms. I kick and scream, but he doesn't let go. He leads me to the gardening shed behind his cabin.

"What the fuck do you think you're doing?" I seethe.

"There's no way in hell I'm going to let you go. Not when I just found you. I'll go find your brother and I'll bring him back, but you're going to sit your sweet ass here until I do."

My eyes go round and I screech, "You're not leaving me here Declan Cain."

"If I asked you nicely would you stay here while I go find your brother?"

"Fuck no!"

"Then you leave me no choice." He unlocks the shed and shoves me inside before I'm able to squeeze passed him. Then he slams the door in my face. I hear the padlock click shut before I start screaming bloody murder. His protective side isn't looking so hot right about now.

When I finish describing all the ways in which I'm going to eviscerate him when I'm free, I manage to get my anger under control. *There has to be a way out of here.*

Light filters in through the cracks in the boards and I hope there aren't any spiders or other creepy crawlies as I wade through the junk on the counters. I come across a small lighter and give a little cry of victory.

I cup the lighter in my hands and flick it to life. The light doesn't do much, but it's enough to see a few inches more than I had and that was going to have to be enough. The plywood counters are jammed full of fishing crap, which won't do me any good. I find a bottle of some kind of accelerant and I stick that in the back of my pants in case I need to burn my way out of here. I'd rather go down in a blaze of glory than be stuck here while my brother is in trouble.

The counters don't prove helpful, so I get down on my knees and crawl around the baseboards, hoping for a gap big enough for me to squeeze through. I give a cry of triumph when I find a patched spot with a piece of plywood. If I'm able to bust the wood off, it should be just big enough for me to squeeze through.

I shove the lighter into my pocket and crouch down under the counter. I lay on my back in the dirt and kick the plywood with both feet. It splits down the middle with a satisfying crack. A few more solid kicks and I'm able to peel the wood the rest of the way off the walls. Chunks cling to the sides and the corners, but screw it.

I get down on my belly and slither in the dirt. I slide one arm though because trying to fit both of my shoulders through would never work. Then I fit my head through the hole, followed by the other shoulder. I grab handfuls of grass and use them to pull my body the rest of the way through.

Covered in dirt, a couple hundred spider webs and grass stains, I stalk into the forest. The early evening light throws shadows all around me, but unlike the previous night, I'm no longer scared of them. My brother is in danger and that's the only thing that matters.

Urgency causes me to pick up the pace. I twist in all directions trying to find a sign of Sam or Declan. I'm jogging by the time the clearing where the tornado hit comes into view. I'm so focused on seeing through the half-light and foliage that I don't see the big ass hole in front of me until it's too late.

The next thing I know I'm airborne, then I land awkwardly on my ankle, the sharp pain shooting up my leg. I crumple, falling sideways to try and take the weight off of it. The light from the lighter does little to illuminate the area so I curl into a ball, my sinuses tingling in an effort to keep the tears of pain and panic at bay.

The tell-tale sound of footsteps sends ice shooting through my veins.

Chapter Fourteen
Sully

The sound of footsteps comes to a halt and I hear someone or something rustling in the grass at the top of the hole. I cower against the earthen wall, my ankle throbbing, my entire body shaking with the adrenaline coursing through my system.

Red peeks his head over the corner and I feel faint with relief. "Oh my God. Oh my God, I'm so glad it's you."

He kneels down, flashing his flashlight around the hole. "What did you get yourself into here?"

I hold up the lighter and he jumps backward, holding a hand up to his face. "I have no idea, but I'd be eternally grateful if you could help me get out of this. I have to find Declan."

"Don't worry. We'll find him," Red says.

"Thank you, thank you, thank you," I yell. "You wouldn't happen to have a rope or something that you could throw down here, do you? Or, if you think you could reach, I'll grab ahold of your hand and pull myself up."

"I don't have any rope and I'm not sure if these old bones would be of much use to you. Why don't you just sit tight while I find Declan?" he asks.

"No!" My fingers pull at the exposed roots and slick mud, hoping for a foothold. "Please don't leave me here. I have to find Declan. My brother is out here somewhere and I can't let them get hurt. You have to help me!"

He moves with shocking speed, dropping to his knees and gripping the lip of the hole with his fingers. His face is gaunt in the light of the moon and I don't know if it's the cast of shadows or the tilt of his lips, but his face has taken on a menacing air. That suspicion is confirmed when he says, "Silly girl. No one is going to help you. Just like no one helped me."

My brain trips over itself as it attempts to comprehend what Red is saying. He circles around the hole which makes me feel increasingly dizzy. I manage to get my bearings and then I notice the blood on his clothes and the deep scratch on his face.

"What happened to you?" I whisper.

"Now that's a good question," he says, his lips spreading into a sinister grin. "One I think you should know since it involves your kin, after all." My brow furrows as he continues. Then realization dawns and I wish I could forget everything that he's saying. "Fifteen years ago, Declan, his mom, dad, and me took a group of folks on a routine hunt. The winter was harsh that year, but there was a herd that made for good game. It wasn't supposed to be a big thing. Just a few days in, a few days out. Piece of cake. We didn't expect the storm. The snowfall was unreal. It was the worst winter storm Indiana had ever seen. And we were stuck right in the middle of it with no way out."

I can't help but think about a fourteen-year-old Declan being stuck in the woods during the middle of a snowstorm where he must have watched as his father died. I think of the somber man who gave me the shirt off his back to keep me warm, the man that took me on the most romantic date of my life just to impress me. Tears spill down my cheeks because I know Red isn't telling me these things to save me.

He's telling me because he knows that I'm right where he wants me.

"There was an accident," Red recalls. "Some members of the group were injured when one of the trees snapped from the weight of snow and ice. It trapped a couple of them, myself included. Declan's daddy was one of the trapped ones and your Poppa Joe. I would have never made it out alive. Not with the temperatures dropping the way they were, but Declan was special. That boy was fast and strong like you wouldn't believe." Red leers at me. "Though I suppose you're pretty acquainted with him now aren't you? Anyway, we sent Declan in the direction of town, though we all knew none of us would be alive by the time he brought help back.

"We were there for three days total. Do you know what that does to a man? The fear of death. A slow, agonizing death. You reach a point where you'll do just about anything to stay alive. You'll make hard decisions. Take lives. Anything. Kill or be killed," he murmurs, looking off into the distance.

"What did you do?" I ask, though I have a sickening feeling in the pit of my stomach that says I don't want to know. But I have to. For Poppa Joe. For Declan and his dad. If I'm going to have any hope of getting all of us out of these woods alive I need to know exactly what we're dealing with.

He turns back to me, eyes red and flat. "By then we were sure Declan hadn't made it out of the storm alive. It was just me, James, and Joe who remained. The others had died. Exposure and the like. The three of us were used to roughing it so we managed as best we could. It wasn't enough. Nothing we could have done would be enough."

My chest heaves as the sense of dread grows. I can't look away from him even though I want to.

"I ate Joe first." I stumble backwards and press my back against the cold dirt wall as he continues, "I managed to get free of the tree, but my leg was lame and I wasn't going to go anywhere on a bum leg. Not trapped like we were and freezing to death on top of it. After Joe, well, I was just so hungry. Even hungrier than I had been before. I couldn't eat enough. Thought I would die from the pain. James was out of it by then, nearly gone from the cold, so I ate him, too. But by then, I really started to enjoy it." He speaks the last few thoughts like he's relishing a fond memory, licking his lips and smiling a little, even.

At that, I lose my battle against the churning nausea in my stomach and vomit on the dirt floor. Of all the things I'd imagined, this was nowhere on the list. Poor Nonna. Poor Declan. This wasn't even a man anymore, I realize, there is no humanity left at all. This...thing in front of me is a monster.

Red's head snaps up as though he's heard something. My heart thuds in my chest. Is it Declan? On one hand I want him to come, to save me again so that I know he's safe, but on another, I can sense that something is terribly wrong here, and I don't want him to come to my rescue if it is only going to get him hurt. Red is dangerous on a level that I can't begin to comprehend and I'd rather die trying to keep him from Declan than to lose him.

"You stay here, now. I'll be back soon," Red says cryptically. Then I watch as his teeth elongate, his eyes turn a darker blood red, and his skin leeches of all color. He hisses, baring his razor-sharp teeth and I can't restrain the scream that rips through my throat any longer. I throw myself back against the wall, scrabbling to get as far away as possible.

I strain to listen as his footsteps recede into nothingness. When I'm certain he's gone, I get to work trying to escape...again. Roots stick out of the soil and I test each one until I find a sturdy one a few feet above me. I manage to grab onto it and find a foothold in the soil wall with my uninjured foot. I find another, but with my sore ankle it takes everything I have not scream out in pain as I put all of my weight on it.

I repeat the process until I'm able to throw my arms over the lip of the hole. There's a slim-trunked tree a little ways away and I manage to get my arms around the base of it to pull myself the rest of the way out.

My eyes dart around the tree-line, searching for his pale white skin against the darkness. When I see nothing, I get to my feet and limp away from that hellhole. I make it halfway around the clearing when I hear the shouts. I pause and try to quiet my thundering pulse. I hear it again, coming from the door to the cellar which is the only thing remaining of the old tourist center.

I check the clearing for signs of Red. When I don't see any, I dart from the cover of the trees to the cellar door. My ankle gives out just as I reach the door. Leaning heavily against it, I whisper-shout, "Sam! Sam, is that you?"

"Sullivan, thank fucking God," Sam answers.

I find a hefty rock nearby and get to work smashing the lock to the door. It busts free and I rip it off, throwing it somewhere over my shoulder. I throw the door open and launch myself at Sam when he appears in the doorway.

"I'm so sorry," I say. "I'm so sorry I've been such a bitch to you. I'm sorry I shut you out when Mom and Dad died. I'm sorry for every horrible, terrible thing I've ever said to you."

He wraps his arms around me, too. "I should get kidnapped more often," Sam says against my hair.

I pull away long enough to deliver several sharp *thwacks* to his chest. "Don't. Ever. Do. That. Again. Sam. Thomas."

"Trust me, the last thing I want to do is have a repeat of today. What the fuck was that thing?"

I shake my head against his chest. "Something. I don't know...something else. This is the weirdest fucking town," I say. "First there's bear shifters, now freaky creatures with weird eyes that eat humans."

"Wait, they have bear shifters, too?" he asks in alarm. "And who eats humans?"

My brow furrows and I release Sam from the hug. "What do you mean they have bear shifters, too?"

"That...thing. Whatever it is. When it found me at Declan's place, it brought me here and tied me up before putting me in the cellar. I watched it chase a wolf that turned into a woman. I know that sounds crazy, trust me, I'm not on drugs or anything, but I watched it with my own eyes. Then it killed it and ate it. With its bare hands. When it was done it was faster, way faster, than before. It fucking ran around on all fours. Maybe I am going crazy, but it looked like it was turning into a wolf, too."

I think about Declan and how fast and strong he is. How quickly he was able to heal after I bandaged him up.

Then I realize that Red had the chance to kill both Sam and I and he didn't. He isn't after us. We're human.

He is after Declan.

Chapter Fifteen
Sully

"We have to find him," I say.

But Sam is already shaking his head, his eyes wide. "The hell we do. If he's a fucking *bear* he can take care of himself. I mean *what the fuck,* Sully? First I find out that you're a wizard or some shit and now you're dating a zoo animal?" I start to object, but he cuts me off. "You bet your ass we're going to talk about that. Later. What we need to do now is get the fuck out of these woods before fuck-face gets back and changes his mind about having us for dinner, if you know what I mean."

"I'm not going to leave him here, Sam, just like I wouldn't leave you here. Now c'mon. We have to find Declan before Red does. If you're right and he's killing shifters to absorb their powers, he could be stronger than Declan now. And if that's the case, he may not have much time."

I peer around the clearing, but I can't see much in the distance. Swift River National Forest is huge. So big that Declan could be anywhere by now.

"Why even take us in the first place?" Sam asks. "I mean if he doesn't eat regular humans, then why even go to the trouble to take me or trap you?"

My body freezes and I turn to face Sam, whose face has also frozen mid-question, the both of us coming to the same conclusion.

"We're bait," I whisper and I nearly heave what little contents I have in my stomach all over my shoes.

"Keep it together for fuck's sake. We have to get out of here."

That manages to snap me out of my fear. I remember the can of accelerant in my back pocket when I hear the thunder of feet racing toward us. My heart stops and I forget the horror in front of me for the one on its way. Declan appears in the tree-line, his body in bear form. Dark fur covers his visible skin, his muzzle longer, and his teeth sharper and more deadly. He's huge normally, but this way he's nearly eight feet of pure, powerful muscle and claws.

When his eyes land on me the sound of his growl

fills the night air. Behind me I hear Sam whisper, "Holy shit he really is a fucking bear."

My mind races, but every scenario I envision ends with someone I love dying, and I can't bear to lose anyone else. And what a hell of a time to realize that I've fallen for him. For this beast I get to call my own. If we make it through this, I vow that I'll make sure he knows it every day for the rest of our lives.

By the time he reaches me, he looks more bear than human. I manage to throw my hands around his throat. His claws come around my back. "Please, we have to go, Dec. Let's go now. It's not safe here."

"Didn't I tell you to stay in the shed? What the fuck are you doing out here?"

"Like I was going to let you go in here alone. We're in this together, remember?" I kiss the fur covering his jaw, cupping it in my hands to feel what he's thinking. I see my face in his mind and hear his responding growl. There's no way he's going to let this go. Hopelessness unfurls, a putrid reminder of our gruesome fate if we take one misstep. "Please," I beg, "please let's just go before something else bad happens."

Sam joins us. "C'mon man. We can talk about it back at your place."

A sound above me catches my attention. Like the

sound of a thousand people all whispering at once. My heart thuds dully in my chest and my hands grow clammy. I look up and come face to face with the thing that had once been a man named Red.

I scream again, the sound echoing through the space. This time when I stumble backward, Sam is there to catch me.

Red is no longer the big-boned red-headed man who I met at Declan's shop. His meaty arms and tree-trunk thighs have melted, shifted, into needle thin limbs wrapped in gray, pockmarked skin. What had once been a large barrel chest is now sunken in and mottled with dark blue bruises. The clothes he was wearing are long gone. The red hair which inspired his nickname is gray, blood-matted and falling off in clumps.

He hangs upside down from one of the tree limbs, his blood-red mouth nearly even with my head. Congealed matter drips from the corner of his mouth and his lips are split wide—nearly ear to ear and house a mouth of razor sharp teeth.

Sam pulls me backwards as the Red-*thing* releases its hold and walks down the tree horizontal to the ground as if it can defy gravity. It stands face to face with me and I search blindly for something to protect ourselves with and come up empty-handed.

Declan growls and I watch as he shifts completely into his bear form; the one that he was so worried would hurt me. If we weren't in such a dire situation I would have admired how beautiful he is. As it is, I barely have time to give his new form a once-over before he's charging at the wraith-like figure of Red.

"Any ideas?" Sam asks, his fingers nearly bruising with their hold on my arms.

I pull out the lighter and accelerant. "When I lit this back in the hole, he seemed afraid of it. What about we pin him in somewhere. Maybe light fires around them so that he can't run away or get loose."

"The fucker can practically fly, Sully, I'm not sure how much a coupla small fires are going to do."

I shake the bottle of accelerant. "Fine, then I'm going to douse him with this and then light him up." I grab a stick and tear off a piece of my shirt. I wrap it around the end and wet it with a couple drops of the accelerant. "Take this and start making fires around them to fence them in. I'll do the same on this side. I don't want this son-of-a-bitch getting away."

Sam drags the torch around in a circle. I start to go in the opposite direction. Hopefully, Red will stay busy with Declan long enough that he doesn't notice what we're up to.

Declan's bear form stalks the thin white figure over the grass. His powerful jaws snap and growl as Red leads him on a winding pattern, taunting him like he taunted me the night of the tornado. That must be part of the thrill for him now; frightening his victims before he goes in the kill. Tenderizing his prey.

I race around the circle until I meet Sam on the other side. Declan lunges at Red, his teeth reaching for his outstretched arm. Red manages to evade, almost like he's not even trying. My heart sinks when I realize that this is all just a game to him.

My fear that this is going to end badly causes me to take a few steps backward, then I take a running leap and jump over the fence of flames and to the other side.

"Hey, asshole!" I shout, catching the attention of both bear and monster.

Declan objects with a growl and the monster turns to Declan and his lips spread wide in a mocking smile. But that's his fatal error. The one second of distraction allows Declan to leap for his throat, ripping it out with one powerful bite. The moment Red takes his attention off of Declan, I start to run toward them, legs pumping as fast as I can make them go.

Red falls to the ground, black blood spitting out of the fatal wound in his neck, his fingers clutching at the wound to stave the flow. Without giving myself a moment to think about my actions, I drench what's left of his body with the accelerant and flick the lighter to life. Red lifts one bony arm toward me before I drop the lighter on his emaciated body. It sparks to life like tinder, black smoke curling for the sky, but never quite dissipating. It gathers above his body like a thick cloud, then it drifts towards the ground, before disappearing into the soil.

Epilogue
Declan

One Year Later

I lock up the shop, smiling as I hear Sully's cheerful voice a few feet down the road at the office to the *Chronicle*. She's wearing one of those cute little summer dresses that I like so much. Which is a shame because it's probably going to get dirty. And she'll probably get pissed and go off on me. The beast inside me growls and I flex, trying to tamp down my own excitement. The both of us would do well to learn a little restraint. But damn if it doesn't make me hard when she gets all pissed off.

After I pocket my keys, I head down the street toward her. She looks up, catching my eye and smiles. She makes her excuses with her coworkers and lifts up to her toes to press a kiss against my lips.

"I thought you were tired of working for the Chronicle," I say, as I lead her back toward the shop.

"You know, I think I judged it unfairly in the beginning. I kind of like having my fingers in everything in this town. I like knowing everything before everyone else."

"Oh you do, do you?"

"Yes, I do. Don't tell anyone, but I may or may not have seen that Leroy is thinking of giving me a paid internship for senior year." She holds up her hands in triumph. "No more Cup-o-noodles!"

As she's gotten more used to her gift this year, she's learned how to control it. Sometimes she even lets herself have a little innocent fun with it. "I'm proud of you, baby."

"Thank you. So where are you taking me? It's the anniversary of our first date, mister man. I hope you have something special up your sleeve."

"I do, but I'm not sure you're going to like it."

"I'm sure I'm going to love it."

The river that runs by the shop is as clear as glass. My boat waits by the dock where I had Sam tie it up earlier. He's proven to be a shark when it comes to sales. I've never had so many female customers. At first I thought hiring him on to replace Red was a mistake, but the constant ca-ching of my register disagrees.

"We're going somewhere in the boat?" she asks.

I hold her hand to help her in. "We're going fishing," I tell her.

Her smile fades. "Fishing?"

I try to keep mine from showing as I untie the line. "That's right."

"With worms?"

"I'll even teach you how to bait them."

"This isn't exactly what I had in mind when I said a romantic evening, Dec."

"I think worms are very romantic."

"Well, you're also delusional."

I steer the boat down the river and smile at her. "Only with you," I say. "Besides we were interrupted the first time I tried to take you."

Sully goes quiet at the reminder of what we survived and then asks, "Do you ever think about it?"

The river is quiet today and the sun burns bright overhead warming my skin. "Not a day goes by that I don't." Especially days like this when I'm out on the river, doing things that Red, my father and I had done together hundreds of times before. "But I know that thing wasn't him. It was something else. Something evil. It's like he was cursed because of what he did."

"I'm just sorry you had to lose another person you cared about."

I lift her chin with a finger. "Don't be. I am finally able to put my past to rest. My parents, what happened to them, I never thought I'd get past it because I felt responsible. But I know there are some things that I can't control and they would want me to be happy."

"And are you?" she asks, even though she's learned to read my human form.

Instead of answering, I pull her into a kiss, sinking into her familiar taste with a growl of approval inside my head. She smiles against my lips and wraps her arms around my shoulders. I could spend forever with her in my arms.

I pull away and kiss her forehead. "Don't think you can distract me. It's going to happen."

She eyes the tackle box dubiously, but I know for a fact she's going to enjoy what's inside. I spent the past two weeks going back and forth with Suzanna to make sure today would be perfect. From Sully's mother's diamond ring to her favorite flower.

She just has to bear with me a little longer.

Acknowledgments

To my Knockouts for being beside me every step of the way. A special shout-out to Ella Stewart, Elle Vanzandt, Teri Hicks, Catherine Hayward, and Lori Vandenburg for their eagle eyes.

To Mia Searles for her everlasting support and friendship. And for my rad birthday present. You rule.

Vanessa from PREMA Romance. I thank you for your tutelage, cheerleading, and willingness to sit through my plot interrogations and painstakingly wading through my word vomit and turning it into gold.

To Afton, always. I love you!

About the Author

 **Nicole Blanchard** is the *New York Times* and *USA Today* best-selling author of gritty romantic suspense and heartwarming new adult romance. She and her family reside in the south along with their two spunky Boston Terriers and one chatty cat. Keep up-to-date on her new releases by subscribing to her newsletter.

Also by Nicole Blanchard

First to Fight Series

Anchor

Warrior

Valor

Box Set: Books 1-3

Survivor

Savior

Honor

Box Set: Books 4-6

Traitor

Operator

Aviator

Captor

Protector

Armor

A Salvation Society Crossover: Reckless

Friend Zone Series

Friend Zone

Frenemies

Friends with Benefits

Box Set

The Lost Planet Series

The Forgotten Commander

The Vanished Specialist

The Mad Lieutenant

Journey to the Lost Planet (Books 1-3)

The Uncertain Scientist

The Lonely Orphan

The Rogue Captain

Return to the Lost Planet (Books 4-6)

The Determined Hero

The Arrogant Genius

The Runaway Alien

Saving the Lost Planet (Books 7-9)

Dark Romance

Toxic

An Immortal Fairy Tale Series

Deal with the Dragon

Vow to the Vampire

Kiss from the King

Standalone Novellas

Bear with Me

Darkest Desires

Mechanical Hearts